SOMETHING FOUND: *A Coin*

TROY AARON RATLIFF

COPYRIGHTED MATERIAL

Copyright ©2020 by Troy Aaron Ratliff
Cover and art Copyright © 2020 by Damonza.com
Formatting by Damonza.com; Edited by Mike Robinson

ISBN: 9798681931058

This is a work of fiction. Any names, characters, places, and incidents are either products of the author's imagination or used fictitiously. Any resemblance to actual events, locales, or persons, living or dead, is entirely coincidental.

All Rights Reserved.

No part of this publication can be reproduced or transmitted in any form or means, electronic or mechanical, without permission from the author.
Patreon.com/troyaaronratliff
#SomethingFound
First Edition

OTHER WORKS:

Novels:

Do I Bother You At Night?

Short Stories:

High Bridge

Going Down

The Uninvited Guest

Little Bernie's Map

Just Past The Trees

For my brother

You are truly missed—

COURAGE

Against the Past

BOOK I:
A COIN

PROLOGUE

From *The Citizen* newspaper, Key West, Florida:

Tribute Paid to Good Samaritan Local Artist

Todd Freeman, so-called "Selfless Scavenger", receives local award, celebration outside his art gallery.

By Abigail Prine
Citizen Staff Writer

The old schoolyard adage "Finder's Keepers" doesn't exactly fit Todd Freeman's worldview.

Standing in the afternoon sun outside the art gallery he has owned and operated for the past three years, he takes time to acknowledge the tourists and locals who pause to watch the low-level celebration taking place there – even as he is the center of it.

Pictures are taken. Hugs and handshakes go 'round. And applause breaks out when Mayor Michelle Smith herself hands none other than the Florida Keys Humanitarian Award to this scruffy artist dressed in cargo shorts and a tropical shirt.

Indeed, Todd – a transplant from Ohio – is the most casual present: and in Key West, that's saying something.

Yet beyond what some might assume is a bronzed bohemian-type lies Todd's deeper nature, what one woman called his "angelic generosity". Another coined the term "Selfless Scavenger". We here at *The Citizen* thought the latter had a nice ring to it, so, as regular readers might know, we've adopted the tag.

Todd's reputation as an artist grew alongside his reputation as a discoverer (or *recoverer*) of lost things. The beach doesn't lack for folks scoping with metal detectors, but few have woven themselves so indelibly into the fabric of the community. Part of Todd's distinction is his keen eye for objects others might well just ignore.

"It is Magical," he told me, when discussing the influence of Key West on his art, which runs the gamut from sunset canvases to floral wood engravings. "And I hope if you print that it's capitalized."

"Magical?" I ask. "Why is that?"

"It's a respect thing," he says. "Sure, everywhere has a dark history. Nowhere is perfect, but some places certainly fit some people much better than others, and if it fits you right, the Magic will be obvious. It's like a calling."

No doubt, Todd himself even has a footprint in that "dark history": almost two years after his conviction, the name Jeremy Patrick still sends chills down the collective Key West spine just as Andrew Cunanan's or Samuel Little's names still do in Miami. As we know, though, the killer's reckoning began not in the hands of detectives, but in the routine escapades of our local Selfless Scavenger. When scouring one day, Todd stumbled across what proved to be the case's crucial piece of evidence: the crowbar stained with the blood of Patrick's 21-year-old victim, Kimberly Lawson.

According to Todd, his work was never purposefully about sleuthing or crime-solving. It has always been about returning lost treasures, as any astute reader may guess from his section of our website, where for the last six months he has listed the trinkets, valuables, toys, knick-knacks, and other items he's uncovered exclusively with us.

When asked about his feelings on receiving the Florida Keys Humanitarian Award, Todd replies, "It feels really good to be recognized, but... I'd hope I'm not unique. I would hope anyone can relate to someone who's lost something precious or irreplaceable, anything from a priceless item to a daughter like Kimberly [Lawson], or a son." For the briefest of moments, his gaze lowers.

"With me," he continues, "it's three-ways selfish. I get the high of discovery, I get the high of reuniting people with their lost things, and I get the high of inspiration from it all, for my art. That's a win all around to me."

Todd's accrued no shortage of nicknames over the years: the Selfless Scavenger, as noted, The King Solomon of Key West, the Scruffy Angel, the Angel Artist, the Angel of Key West, the Scruffy Sympathetic Scribbler, among many others. So, which one does he prefer?

Todd pauses at this, seeming to take the question quite seriously. "They all make me sound so... legendary," he says.

"Don't you mean Magical?" I asked.

Todd laughed. "As long as it's capitalized."

CHAPTER 1

SCOURING

THE SCHWINN CLICKED like a fishing line as he navigated the edge of the tropical neighborhood. Blades of late afternoon sun cut through the swaying palm trees. His sifter, mini-shovel and fanny pack clanked together, the chorus of his daily routine against the caw of the gulls and the hush of the waves. Todd Freeman glided to his favorite post to lock up his bike: right where the street, sidewalk, and beach converged. He thought he smelled grilled Mahi-Mahi on the wind.

Todd clutched the metal detector in one hand and rolled the old bike past Mrs. Renee's plant-covered porch. He didn't see her for their customary wave, but he got his first extra strong whiff of beach air, salty as the rim of a glass and blown right into his face, overpowering the brief hint of grilled fish.

He spotted a couple walking away from the water after what Todd presumed was an overstayed visit, given the lobster redness of their skin. Even from his distance he knew they'd be hurting bad by tomorrow.

They took notice of him. He hopped off the bike and walked it to the favorite weathered and initial-scrawled post, watching them. By the time they got close enough, he had already locked the bike and readjusted his tool belt.

Todd offered them a smile.

The couple, a middle aged guy whose face told the world he never wanted to go to the beach again in his life only took a quick glance at him, while a plump, short-haired woman who followed, offered a kind smile in return. He was more on a march, hauling their beach chairs and a beach bag while she followed behind in an open-armed waddle, more for her burned skin than her size, her hands raised and swinging with each step, as if she was walking on stilts.

Holding his smile, Todd said, "Hello."

"'Ello" The woman said in a soft and reedy British lilt. "Windy day today."

"Yeah? Sunny too?" Todd asked, hoping he didn't come off as too sarcastic to her.

"Oh! Like you wouldn't believe!" she exclaimed, the *eeeve* stretching out in her voice for emphasis.

Todd waited for her to pass through the small walkway to and from the sands. As he did, she noticed his gear.

"Wassat you got there?" she asked, and pointed.

"Oh, what? My metal detector?"

"Yeah, I 'adn't seen one of those in years. You a treasure hunter?"

"Hmm. More or less."

"You look like one. Especially with that belt."

"Tools of the trade." Todd slipped past her as he noticed a thin gold chain slathered against her sweaty sun-reddened chest.

"You ever find anything *big*? Like...*reeeeally* big?"

"Uh, to me, it depends on who's asking. What's big to you may not be big to the next person."

"So that's a 'no'?"

"Well, you might've left the matching earrings that go with that necklace back at your campsite, and I may find them."

The woman looked liked she had been goosed. Gasping, her

face lit up with surprise and recall, touching her ears. Then she looked to, and rushed toward, the man with the bag and chairs in tow.

"Did you grab my earrings?" *Eeeeariiiings.* Her voice echoed down the street as she tried to catch up to him, sunlight hitting her between the homes and trees.

Faraway, clearly annoyed and very clearly not British, the man called back, "They're in the car, Bernice!"

Todd watched them go, hitching up his belt and his machine. Switching the metal detector from his right hand to his left, he looked at his ring finger on his left hand and the absence of a ring there. Still felt strange, even after all this time…

Reaching the sands, he leaned the machine against his favorite palm tree on the beach and slipped on his headphones. Jacking the corded earmuffs into the machine, he turned it on, and adjusted it.

Then, he set off.

*

The phrase that most of us are familiar with goes, *One man's trash is another man's treasure.* Other variants of that antiquated phrase read differently to some extent or another, but for Todd Darren Freeman of Key West, Florida, he recognized the standard form of that commonplace expression and dwelled on its meaning, as well as just the sounds of the words themselves. Why? Because Todd was the kind of man that used words as solace, who dealt with pain through artistic, creative expression. He was the kind of man who discovered an unmatched meditative quality in the art of a simple, fine-cut phrase.

Nevertheless, like any forward-thinking creative on the prowl for inspiration—not too different from his hunt presently on the beach—he had gone in search of something similar, profound, touching; a phrase for the long haul. Still waters certainly ran deep within Todd, but he believed there was nothing wrong with a cresting wave now and again to wrinkle the surface or a skipping stone to liven things up. To acquire something with the same kind of power that could move him as much as that ordinary expression—a poem, a string of notes from a beautiful song, or perhaps even another famous phrase—was a daunting challenge. So, in the meantime, that proverbial, household adage always came back to him as the most powerful and applicable for him. Powerful enough, in fact, for him to center the better part of his life on the essence of those seven little words.

Todd knew that if this small but weighty serving of himself ever got out, people would counter—with him being an artist and all—that something along the lines of *A picture paints a thousand words* would be more fitting for a man like him; a man with his level of talent and skill.

Nah, no thanks. That one *was* a bit too mainstream for him.

Okay. George Bernard Shaw's line, *Life isn't about finding yourself. Life is about creating yourself* always struck a certain moving cord with Todd, especially with that little seven letter F-word snuck in there, that he adored so much. And that C-word in there, too. The two major pillars of his life, and therefore, a serious contender. Admittedly, Todd never dreamed he would have or *could* have constructed or created a life like his. It was a lifestyle he'd fallen into the way some folks fall unreflectively into homes or careers.

All right, perhaps something equally touching from Van Gogh like, *The more I think about it, the more I realize there is nothing more artistic than to love others*. Todd thought that was pretty apropos, and a hard-running contender for a man who did what he did with his spare time, beyond his painting.

Sometimes, Todd didn't think of himself as an artist at all, but rather a connoisseur of junk piles and lost things. He knew it was incredibly silly. Dusty antiques were not the man's bread and butter, and neither were the things he uncovered beneath the sands of the beaches he would visit. As a matter of fact, they weren't even real interests of his. No, it was the *act* of finding and the humble *deed* of returning in which Todd took the most pleasure. Painting was his income. Painting fed him, physically, emotionally and creatively, on deep levels of his soul. But it was finding and returning that made him feel wealthy. Magical.

Alive.

Suffice it to say, Todd Freeman was welcomed with open arms at any doorway he darkened throughout the southern Florida Keys. The local churches were proud of him, mothers swore they would love to see their sons grow to become a man like Todd, and even the local government—the county of Monroe *and* the city of Key West—beamed that they were the home of such a fine human being, as humanitarian awards and nominations were no stranger to Todd Freeman's name.

Some of the locals unaware of Todd's reputation would think, *There goes another coin shooter, another beach bum just trying to survive*, and feel a trace of pity for him, believing he was a poor man in search of some spare change to buy a cold drink and shelter from the hot sun. Mercy to those unfortunate souls. As Todd swung his metal detector in front of him now, like an invisible and excited dog on the end of its steal leash, making sure to cover all ground, he spotted a few remaining people on the beach peer at him in either that familiar pity or mere curiosity.

Now, depending on the weather and how many tourists decided to invade the Keys during any particular season like hungry ants to a picnic, it was common knowledge to most natives of the Southern 'Conch Islands' that they could find Todd scouring the sands of Higgs, Smathers, and Ft. Zack Beach just before sunset. Sometimes, even relatively smaller beaches on the island like Rest Beach and South Beach were combed, where he usually spotted more Cuban coins, and which offered a nice change in scenery.

Something Found: A Coin

But usually those three main beaches were his standard go-tos, mainly because they were enough to keep him busy. Often, if anyone happened to catch his attention as he swept the sand with his trusty long-necked metal detector, they would send him a wave and a smile, which Todd would answer with his crooked grin that stretched his scruffy face, and lifted his sand-scratched sunglasses. Then he'd continue on, swinging and rotating his detector, the balmy breezes swirling his golden hair as nearby the waves whispered enchanted nothings to the shore. Some remarked that his life could exist on a postcard.

Some also said the postcard could be labeled, *Welcome to Paradise.*

*

With the southern trade winds momentarily calm, and most of the beachgoers packing up for the evening (off to find better digs, no doubt, for the daily Sunset Celebration on the western side of the island) the beach was mostly his own.

There were a few stragglers left behind, some old salty dogs from the nearby Naval Base puffing on expensive cigars or young vacationers reveling in the water's glowing colors, but they were few and far between, and hardly a nuisance.

In reality, Todd's beachcombing was for others as well as himself. People often left pieces of themselves behind in these sands, things for him to find and return. Obviously, misplaced dimes and quarters weren't the makings of sleepless nights, but a lost wedding band or a handsome-looking watch, gifted, say, by a beloved, late grandparent, *was.*

His system was easy. After a find of some potential worth, Todd would jump on the web and make a posting, or do it the old-fashioned way and inform his contact at *The Citizen*, the local newspaper of Key West, of his discovery. With a grain of hope in his heart that someone was looking for the lost object, Todd

Freeman would tell the world what pearl he'd found in this expansive oyster.

So, as a precaution, Todd would keep the findings untouched in a safe place in the back office of his art studio. That is, until he received The Call, when he'd hear the quivering, hopeful voice on the other end, full of tentative optimism for reclaiming their lost treasure.

Over the past few years of trolling the beaches with his Matrix M6 metal detector swaying at his feet, and the headphones mounted on his skull producing that steady, heart rate-monitor beeping, his skin had bronzed to the color of a ripe peach. His hair had a bleached, sandy blonde shade with a soft dotting of gray at his temples, which the sun could also take credit for with a little help from Father Time, none of which took away from his sharpness, and sharp he was.

How sharp? Sharp enough to know that people were aware of the things they'd lost, and understood that losing something dear can be enough to break a person if it has enough significance, enough history, enough *substance*. And it was for this exact reason he advertised his findings.

Granted, he also knew people were going to be people. The darker side of human nature would inevitably raise its ugly head out of the sand with the swindlers and crooks just as alive in their dishonesty as he was in his generosity. But by relying on his instincts, Todd could usually read if they were being honest with him about the lost possessions. The smiles, the reactions, the wide eyes, and various bits of knowledge and events that were connected to the object at hand, were usually enough to tell. Sometimes it was just their glow of hope that he instantly identified when they would creep cautiously through the front door of his studio gallery.

For Todd, however, that was *his* true thrill. Seeing the expressions of faint hope that this might really, *really* be their lost possession, and then to witness and experience the bliss that flooded their faces, was all an incredible high. Some slowly came to tears, while others actually burst out crying right in front of him once Todd brought them the lost item. Sometimes it would move and touch him, as well. As a rule, a well-stocked supply of tissues was always available around the studio.

He kept track of his findings too, no matter what they were, in a journal for his own safekeeping. On record this year alone, the Selfless Scavenger had collected for himself over three hundred dollars in lost change on Higgs Beach. The amount of recyclable junk he had uncovered and had hauled to the salvage center in the back of his car was nearly double that amount. All and all, by the end of the year, if he had chosen to do so, he could have saved enough to make a sizable dint in December's mortgage payment, which in this part of Florida wasn't cheap.

Normally, though, he wouldn't bankroll the money for rent. Instead, he would come up with enough at the end of each week to stroll down to Southern Cross or Sloppy Joe's for some onion rings and a couple of cold ones, enjoy an amateur guitar show on stage, and strike up a nice conversation with a visitor from out of town. Saving was Christ's department. Todd Freeman liked to spend and enjoy; Sunshine-Tax and Spend, you could say. A cheap appetizer and a few beers were a reasonable fee for his good deeds, large and small, worthless and priceless.

Over the past few years of hunting, he had scrounged up everything from sea glass, parts of bicycles, *heaps* of aluminum from soda cans, key chains, keys, paperclips, staples, glasses, watches, Matchbox cars, and even a few crowns from teeth. One time he stumbled upon one of the smaller models of iPods buried just beneath the dunes, the initials *R.C.* carved on the back. It didn't work anymore, but still, being the Selfless Scavenger that he was, he posted it anyway. Maybe "R.C." was still out there, after all.

As expected, not everything he found met an owner. He kept another special box set aside in the back of the gallery for such things he couldn't bring himself to give away. He didn't know why he kept the items since they were junk to him. He only knew *someone* missed them—a broken pocket-watch, a handmade doll with a sad smile stitched on the face with blue button eyes, and even a gnarled necklace with a single shark tooth.

Someone missed them. They were all meant for someone.

After all, one man's trash *is* another man's treasure.

*

Beep-beep-beep.

On this particular balmy, screen-saver of a day in mid-September, between when the last of the college kids had trickled back to school and the snowbirds flew south for the winter—Todd hadn't scrounged up but a few pennies and a beer bottle cap.

There were plenty of days Todd rounded up nothing more than what was currently jingling in his pockets, and there were more than enough days that his searches came up with nothing at all.

Beep-beep-beep.

To anyone who has ever had it happen to them, the feeling that naturally accompanies it is a surreal, almost out-of-body experience. The Rush of Possibility. His hand would brush away the loose sand to see, with his own eyes, what he had discovered, hidden and sparkling and trod over by so many others. It might only be as small as a quarter (or an actual quarter), or perhaps as posh as a gold bracelet, but it was still that King Tut-High, that Montezuma's Gold-Ecstasy that couldn't be equaled.

Beep-beep-beep.

It was closing in on 7:30 in the evening. In fact, it was right around the time when the rest of the country was coming home from another day of work, settling in with their families, eating dinner, or finishing up *Wheel of Fortune* and preparing their tired minds for a grueling round of *Jeopardy!* (a favorite of Todd's when rainy weather held him indoors, or the call of the sands was lacking).

Beep-beep-beep.

It was about ten feet from the shore, right about where the dry sand met wet, and it was understandable that no one spotted it since it looked like a weathered shell with rough edges, or maybe another old rusted bottle cap.

*Beep-be-EP-BEEP-**BEEP-BEEP!***

He stopped, then reached for the little gardening shovel hanging from his belt.

Todd had picked up tips about maximizing the treasure hunting experience, and couldn't help but smile each time he slipped on his utility belt for a trip to the beach or when he reached for one the tools hanging from his hips. Although, they did feel like more than just tools for his trade. No, they felt more…*superhero* to him, silly as that might sound. His own personal utility belt. The adult equivalent of his old Batman pajamas.

About ten days before, when he'd been working on a canvas of brilliant red hibiscus in bloom, and of course with his signature pink and blue Key West villas subtly keeping watch in the background, a category-three hurricane named Eli had come crashing through the Caribbean. Not an end-of-times whopper, but nothing to thumb a nose at either. Eli had slammed Jamaica with one-hundred-and-ten mile an hour winds, killing three people while gaining considerable strength. From there, the storm had weakened to a category two, but only briefly, before suddenly swinging northwest toward Cuba and the Keys, picking up speed once more.

Eli had been the exact kind of storm the snowbirds were so frightened of. This always made Todd laugh, who had lived through several Ohio blizzards, a minor Los Angeles earthquake, and a flood that swept away most of a Mississippi town of less than a thousand residences. Hurricanes *were* frightening; there was no doubt about it (especially when appearing on the Doppler radar during the weather forecast as a massive blob hulking straight for you). Obviously, living in the Keys, you made sure to get the hell out of Dodge when one rolled into town with guns blazing. Yet there was a certain upside to hurricanes for a Selfless Scavenger like Todd Freeman: these storms would bring in wash from the ocean, and sometimes...*sometimes*...the findings were incredible.

Eli had blown through just two weeks ago. In that time, Todd had found a lot of rusted, barnacle-encrusted parts of sunken ships—or so he liked to think—and other random scraps of steel and metal. There was even a misshapen piece of something that he was sure was a warped fragment of a downed plane, a souvenir the ocean had taken for itself that had been wrenched from the trenches of the Gulf Stream and wound up on the shore. He planned to do some investigating over the next few months with the wreckage, perhaps connect it with a plane or a ship that might have gone down in the past few years.

Except, his optimism was overshadowed by his innumerable discoveries in the past that tended to be nothing exciting—nothing to write home about, as the saying goes. Todd secretly knew in his heart this promising airplane scrap would ultimately come to nothing more than junk, but he kept his hope alive that it might be a clue to something bigger. It wasn't like *that* hadn't happened before. Go ask Jeremy Patrick, Prisoner J776GK9.

He could do a little research and see where it took him. Who knew? It might be the keystone to the puzzle that he, and anyone else who was interested, might need to see the whole mysterious picture.

That was what it took to be a connoisseur, was it not? Dedication, integrity, and research.

Yesterday on the beach, he had come up with bones. He assumed the haul Eli had brought in had depleted by this point, although he was finding some nice-looking shells to add to his collection, something he could draw inspiration from for a new painting. He also assumed that was exactly what he was bending down to grab when the metal detector sounded off in such wild insistence.

So when Todd found it…the tiny, weathered disc pressed just a fingernail deep beneath the gritty sand, with the headphones bursting to squealing life, he thought, even with the most minimal amount of luck, that it might be another penny to go in his pocket, and nothing more. Perhaps, it could even be a Cuban or Mexican coin, given the color.

Wiping away the grains of sand, he noticed the item bore the dirty brown color of aged American pennies but was much weightier; like the weight of maybe three Kennedy half-dollars, from his guess.

Todd thought, *Well, that's better than another rusted out piece of scrap.*

Then he examined it closer.

First off, the size was wrong for it to be an average American penny, or even a Mexican peso for that matter. It was the size of a quarter. It easily could have been a quarter floating out in the ocean, all the salts and minerals eating at it for Poseidon knew how many years.

But he doubted it.

Todd wiped some of the last grains of sand from the surface, to expose the face profile engraved there. It *was* a coin—he was certain of that, at least. He pondered for a moment, as his coin expert contact in Miami, Alex, floated into this mind. He wondered what he would think of this one and made a mental note to email him tonight.

He made out the profile of a man on the coin, similar to that of Lincoln on the penny. Only there was something different that Todd could just barely see on the face in the dull orange glow of the setting sun.

He blinked away sweat and turned the coin over in his clammy palm, finding what looked like random, embossed scribbles. The heat was relentless, the sweat stinging his eyes. He squinted, wiping his face against his forearm and then the collar of his shirt.

I'll look at it later, he thought, and stuffed the coin in his fanny pack hanging on the side of his hip. He stood up, glanced around. The beach was empty. A warm breeze off the ocean tussled his hair as large clouds sat bunched across the southern horizon, toward Cuba.

CHAPTER 2

SOUTHERN CROSS

ROWDY SIBLINGS TEND to stay close together, since there is fun in numbers. The geography of the American South is really no different. On Duval St.—Key West's glittering, wild and rambunctious answer to its saucy and chic older brothers, New Orleans' French Quarter, and Miami's own backyard circus of South Beach—Todd owned a small, nameless art gallery. Only a stone's throw from Ernest Hemmingway's former home and current museum, it was a building easily missed. If not for the sheer simplicity of the opened glass display, and by the way it seamlessly blended with the surrounding tropical ambiance, Todd's studio stood out from the *lack* of flamboyance, aglow with a pure, old world, Floridian simplicity.

The one saving eye-catcher, other than the large plate-glass window, was the latest canvas of the week, displayed and framed there for all passing tourists to view. The presentation of a single piece captured the passersby usually for its bold minimalism, in the tradition of, say, Piet Mondrain or even Steve Jobs. Locals who knew of Todd liked to consider whatever painting he chose for the window during any particular week as his comment on the affairs of the world. Sometimes they would debate whether it mirrored Todd's state of mind with reds and crimsons indicating a passion for something, while lavenders were a cool off of issues either exterior or interior to his life. Some neighbors said it was a window into his very soul, visualized through his craft and expression, disclosed to everyone for interpretation.

All of it was fun speculation, of course. Most folks thought they were just pretty pictures. In any case, in spite of the simplicity, his shop stood out on the street. When everywhere you looked there was something to see of some level of garishness, gaudiness, or extreme, the place where there was nothing to see, people's eyes were naturally drawn. It came off as Frank Stella birthed in a sea of Andy Warhol—a blank island void of unfussy artistic expression in an ocean of Pop Art by way of Conch Island and Margaritaville flair.

Or maybe not.

Some of the more astute, even snooty, visitors to Todd's gallery-studio considered it an avant-garde business approach, something of an unconscious ode to composer John Cage's 4'33" composition, applied as a way of standing out by saying nothing at all. In short, they were implying his straightforward work (nonthreatening floral pieces and underwater seascapes were his specialty, usually paired with some charming Key West themed addition), along with his lack of local kookiness, was nothing but an overly minimalistic advertisement; a joke, a hoax, and just an easy—even lazy—way to get attention. That Todd was, to use a Key Westerner's example, a lowly, bobbing buoy in a typhoon of trashiness that was only trying to survive: just as wet as everything else, struggling to float above the rest, but no less a lowly buoy, no matter how you looked at it.

After this nibble of opinion was related to him early on as an artist in Key West, Todd knew two things. The first was the realization he was in way over his head for some of the upper-crust snobs who visited his gallery, and who would schlep their high class Chicago or Manhattan standards (and arrogance) down to the Keys. The other was, after he YouTubed what the hell they were talking about with John Cage and 4'33", Todd thought the individuals who compared a completely soundless orchestra to a meek, reserved art studio needed three things: to get over themselves, a reality check, and a swift kick in the ass that he was more than willing to provide.

The simplicity worked for him.

For the record, Papa Hemingway's former digs had nothing to do with the choice of his studio's location. Although, the museum did bring in some of their stragglers, naturally enticed by the Southern Cross bar next door to him. Todd liked to think the strong drinking spirit of Hemingway himself still haunted the house, possessing the guests and coaxing them in the direction of the nearest watering hole for some exorcizing through the holy redemptive powers of liquid courage.

Todd's studio, a quaint little building that had been in need of a few minor repairs when he stumbled upon it, had come at a fairly cheap price for the area. On top of that, there was a one-bedroom apartment on the second floor that would serve his bachelor needs to a T. The eventual addition of the bar next door seemed to be Ernest subtly blessing his efforts, raising a glass to him from the Great Beyond. Though, he didn't think that initially.

Todd had received many suggestions over the years to set up a margarita bar in studio to complement his Floridian art, to persuade his potential customers into buying some of his work with Blue Hawaiians and Mojitos in their hands to loosen their purse strings from Pickled Brain Syndrome.

"That's not my thing, but I'll consider it." That was always his answer, accompanied with a thoughtful narrowed eye, as if it were the first time he had ever heard that ancient suggestion. Todd was known for his humble, inoffensive paintings featuring seascape settings, colorful floral pieces, and wood art, so he wasn't too sure a rowdy bar and his studio would work well together, not to mention the licensing and risk.

Soon enough though, and with a fair amount of coincidence, the owner of the gift shop next door passed away after a long battle with liver cancer, and business for them began to slip before going out like a weak, wind-whipped flame. Not long after, Todd got word that there were more than a few proprietors vying for the now empty building, with hopes of renovating it into a bar, simply for the opportunity to be next to Todd Freeman's gallery. Todd found out later that it was from the suggestions of people around town that there needed to be booze served with Todd's studio, since Todd wasn't budging on the idea. The combination of the relaxed atmosphere in his place added with a few mixed cocktails would be dynamite, guaranteed.

Within a few weeks, there was a new residence that had set up shop next door. "Southern Cross" was what the weathered wooden marquee read, and with a leaning palm tree and setting sun design carved and painted onto it, the combination brought a number of ideas as to what kind of business they were into. Todd considered if it even *was* a bar, secretly hoping that it wasn't.

But not for very long. No more than a week had passed with Todd half-expecting—with a growing uneasiness—to see glowing Bud Light and Corona signs sprouting up in the back of the darkened interior.

They were there the next day.

*

Davis Sanders was the lucky man who had moved into the vacated building and was the proprietor of Southern Cross. To Todd's surprise, he and Davis struck up a neighborly friendship almost instantly. Southern Cross was just another bar in Key West (and Davis was just another Yankee to the natives in town), but what this particular bar didn't bring was that usual ugly, off-color atmosphere of so many watering holes the world over. Instead of rowdy voices and drunken arguments, there was soft music and quiet conversation.

Todd's concerns of a new dive started to wane. By the first week, Davis had invited him over for a drink on the house, which led to some lively conversation about their northerner's outlook on Florida, which almost always slid back to the warm climate. Two weeks into their neighborly relationship, Todd saw a minor rise in his art sales. And by the end of the first month, Todd and Davis were swapping CDs regularly, seasoning the air on this part of their block with Jimmy Buffet tunes and warm laughter. During the later hours, various couples and groups of young intellectuals would converge long after Todd's nameless little studio was closed and he had ventured off to Sloppy Joe's or to the sack for the evening.

Todd had worried that initial uneasiness of a rowdy neighboring bar into something that he eventually realized wasn't even there. The anxiety, he found, was a ghost of his past. Not *the* ghost, but a fluttering and passing emotional reaction to signs of change.

Hard to argue for a man who had made such major adjustments in his own life not that long ago. But in Todd's old life, change usually spelled bad news. Change meant downsizing, pay cuts, missed chances, missed loved ones, lost love, and the blight of lost opportunities. He had to remind himself that things were different for him now.

They weren't the way they used to be.

Davis was a short, thick man that reminded Todd of Joe Pesci. Davis's demeanor wasn't that of Joe Pesci's normal intense film roles, but was a friendly, witty man with a constant five o'clock shadow and a wheezing laugh, perpetually in pursuit of that Floridian trend of building one's unique, tropical piece of the American Dream—not unlike Todd himself.

Six weeks after they met, Todd and Davis clinked Strawberry

Daquiris, laughing about their bullies from grade school still shoveling snow in their hometowns while they drank and watched the Florida sunset, and all the blazing colors Todd thought only existed in dreams.

*

On this September night, Todd had biked back from the beach with a small handful of things in his leather fanny pack, clinking and rattling as he pedaled, a new addition to the music coming from the tools jingle-jangling on his belt.

That funny penny he had found piqued his interest, and had taken his thoughts to an idea for a new art project that had come to him as he was returning to his bike. Cruising through the dark, muggy street on that second-hand Craigslist-lifted Schwinn, he pondered and played with the idea all the way home. Pulling up to the curb and hearing, yet again, another customary Jimmy Buffet tune over the chatter and laughter of the crowd, he found that Southern Cross next door was filled with its normal share of visitors.

Davis and Todd had joked before about the constant soundtrack of Key West's streets. Could they ever possibly get sick of the sounds of steel drums, live chickens clucking and clicking on cobblestone sidewalks, the whisper of palm fronds in the sea breeze, or faraway motorboats cutting swaths in the glistening water? Hardly, they decided. What was the alternative, after all? Honking bus horns and screaming derelicts? Men of their age knew when to be grateful for what they had. So, whether it was the fearless leader of the Parrotheads, blowing trade winds, Conga, Cuban music, or wind chimes made of clattering coconut shells and bamboo, there was always a rhythm to which people would unconsciously groove.

As Todd glided to the stairs that led to his apartment above the gallery, he noticed Davis's truck was still parked on the street

Something Found: A Coin

in front of Southern Cross, so he knew he was still around. That was strange, but he was thankful. As it was Thursday night, he knew Davis usually headed to the store for his weekly grocery shopping, and Todd hoped to catch a ride with him. He was surprised he hadn't gone already.

Todd hopped off the bike, and rolled it to the white wooden exterior stairs that gripped the side of the gallery and parked it. He left the bike stationed at the bottom of the staircase but took the metal detector, headphones, and effects with him up the stairs. Just inside his door, he left the leather fanny pack on the small end table, where he normally left his keys, cap, and cash, and left the headphones wrapped around the handlebar of the metal detector, propping it against the inside wall.

Returning to his bike at the foot of his stairs, checking to make sure Davis's truck was still there—it was—he then carried that to the entry of his apartment next.

After leaning the bike on the wooden posts of his porch, he two-stepped it back down the stairs, and set off to track down his friend, tapping his pockets for his keys and wallet, making sure he hadn't left those behind.

At the front of the patio of Southern Cross, gazing past the dim lights, he searched for Davis behind the bar. Past the patrons, he noticed a tall, bronzed blonde woman of about twenty-five, slinging drinks. She wore a sassy look that said she owned the place—one that said *she* was the one who had brought in all these customers. With her shirt tied at her middle, exposing her pierced naval and the tribal sun tattoo surrounding it, Todd thought she might very well deserve to wear that sexy little smirk.

Davis wasn't anywhere to be found. Todd had no idea who this current barkeep was, despite having come to know most people that populated Southern Cross. As he entered the patio, he tried to think if Davis had mentioned any new hires in the last week.

Todd was repeatedly astonished by Davis's striking bargirls. It was as if he had some waitlist of gorgeous young women pining to work for him. Todd only talked to them occasionally and didn't know many of them by name, merely for the fact Davis would usually catch Todd before any of the bartenders did and then the free drinks would liberally flow. Cheers, Davis!

Strolling up Southern Cross's cobblestone walkway, Todd could smell the cherry-hinted aroma of a burning cigar. He spotted the source: an out-of-place, lonely-looking city man with designer bifocals and a razor thin goatee, a fog of smoke surrounding him.

Approaching the bar, he met eyes with the cute blonde bartender. She shot him a smile that belonged in a Hooters calendar. No customers were presently at the bar, incredibly, and the bargirl gave Todd her full attention, blue eyes curious and wide, all her teeth white and shining.

"Hi!" she said. "What can I get you, sailor?"

Indifferently, Todd said, "I'm not a sailor, but thanks. Is Davis here?"

The blonde paused, thought, and gave him an exaggerated pout that made Todd cringe a little inside. *Aw, God*, he thought. *Another blonde to give us all a bad name. All she needs to do is make that annoying humming sound to help her think. To help her look playful and flirty. To work that tip out of me. Sorry Sweets, not tonight.*

"Hmm," she cooed, and turned left and then right, looking for Davis. Meanwhile, Todd winced as if struck by sudden pain.

"I don't know where he is," she answered.

Another attractive young woman appeared from the corner of the bar, seemingly out of the darkness. She was someone he actually did recognize: Andrea, the raven-haired Miami U student currently on a Gap Year between college and settling on a career. The tall blonde looked to Andrea, who was equally as pretty, but about five inches shorter. She was hauling a plastic tub with clean, wet shot glasses and beer steins. "Andi, where's Dave?"

Andrea set down the tub of glasses with a clatter and pointed out past the patio, toward the entrance.

Todd followed her finger and saw the blazing red brake lights of Davis's truck. Somehow, Davis had slipped right past him.

Todd thanked the girls and jumped from the bar and headed outside. He began waving his arms when the white reverse lights of the truck illuminated.

"Davis! Yo! Davy!"

In a squeal of brakes, the truck stopped.

Todd ran to the passenger side of the truck, to the open window, as Davis reacted like an enthusiastic drama student to the figure that suddenly appeared there, arms flailing, shouting over the dull rumble of the engine and overreacting like a man about to be pounced by either a werewolf or a velociraptor. Davis screamed in a high-pitched shriek as he threw his arms up in front of his face. As quickly as this exaggerated response was, it disappeared to normal Davis and he offered a casual, "Oh, hey Todd."

Todd was already laughing by the time he reached the truck.

The windows of his vehicle were already down since the air conditioning had stopped working, unfortunately for Davis, right at the start of summer. Davis leaned over the passenger side of the cab for a better look at his neighbor. "What's the word on the street, my man?"

"Hey, Dave. Could I bum a ride to the store?"

"Hop in, mang!" (Davis's way of saying *man* always came out as *mang*, which Todd mercilessly ragged him over), then he played gentleman and scholar by opening the door for him. "Need some milk and sugar, or just the regular supply of jumbo rubbers and tampons?"

Todd laughed. "No, actually, I need a drink."

"Really? Youse?"

Todd nodded. "Stranger things have happened."

*

The idea that had popped in his head earlier in the evening, while pedaling his way back home, the one that he couldn't shake, was now ready to burst out of him. Like any artist and creative will tell you, ideas come and go, but this one could possibly initiate something new and big. He could hear the English woman he said hello to at the beach earlier. *Like, reeeeeally big?*

Yeah, like really big, a seismic shift in his craft and style, even. With all the coins he had found over the years, Todd thought, why not play around with painting them? In the nearly three years they had known each other, Davis was certainly the more masterful at coaxing ideas out of the other. It was why he wanted to run his idea though the filter of a non-artist like Davis.

During their shopping trips, Davis and Todd were two typical men going for supplies: short and to the point. No lollygagging, all business, meeting back at the truck when they were done, but the rides there were usually a different story.

On the way to the store, Davis and Todd would share wild stories of the characters they had met during the week, taking their time getting to the store to fully enjoy and revel in each other's encounters. Davis usually had the lion's share of bizarre anecdotes from the bar crowd that darkened his door. Although, on occasion, the standout tourists who would come to Southern Cross were the very same clowns who had just come from, or were going to, Todd's gallery. It wasn't rare for them to know exactly who the other was talking about right from the start of the conversation, which led, generally, to the same colorful conclusions about certain people.

Tonight was no different. When they reached the parking lot of the Winn-Dixie, the laughs had died down and Davis finally asked "how his art was going."

"I got an idea, actually," Todd said. "Something different."

"Oh yeah? Like what?"

"I've always found the different designs of the same things fascinating. I'm thinking I could make a series of it."

Davis replied with a confused and snappy, "Example." He edged his truck into a spot near the middle of the parking lot, under a tall light post. A woman pushing her shopping cart to the sedan next to them shot them both a leering eye as she popped her trunk.

"Well, you know, like cell phones, or cars or trees," Todd said. "There are so many different designs and styles and looks of the same thing, since, essentially, they're all still a tree, they're all still a phone, all still a car. But they all look so *different*. They all stand out as unique. Well, what if I took that concept and applied it to something like everyday things? Just lining them up across the canvas, or pile them on top of each other? And for the last one in the series, I paint human faces and how different everyone can look, but in essence, they're all still human."

Davis nodded, his bottom lip jutting out. He raised his eyebrows for added effect. This, obviously, gave Todd some hope. "Not bad. I'm not the artsy fartsy guy currently sitting in the truck, but I could see that being nice. I'd buy one." Davis smiled and he put the truck in park and chuckled. "Would you be up to doing beer bottles? *They* have all kinds of different looks, right?"

"For you Davey, anything," Todd said and got out of the truck.

Davis killed the engine and followed suit.

"What did you have in mind to start off this series?"

The twilight air had cooled into the darkness of the evening, but warmth still abided. Todd considered this question with a full, deep breath. "Well, I thought with all the coins I've collected and saved in my jars, I could use money to start off...from Cuba, the Bahamas, Jamaica, and here. Canada. I thought I could put a strange little coin in the middle of it all. One no one has ever seen before. And when I do the human painting, I wouldn't have anyone who stands out at all. Kind of an equality message, you know? Fairness and neutrality, you know?" Then, bluntly, "Does any of this make sense or am I talking out of my ass?"

Davis chuckled as he walked toward the line of shopping carts at the entrance of the market. When Todd turned to him with his question, he thought Davis already had an eye on the one cart he was going to snag. "No, that sounds good, my man. What beer bottle are you going to use for the odd man out?"

"Well…that's where you come in, ol' buddy, ol' pal. Didn't you mention you wanted to start your own brew?" And then Todd softly smacked Davis's arm.

Davis looked at him smugly and chuckled again, following this up with a soft, automatic clap of the hands to show he understood the humor in his seriousness.

Then, unexpectedly, Davis put his hands on his chest in a flamboyant display that caught the eyes of a few departing shoppers. "You're saying that *I*, the lowly and mortal Davis Reilly Sanders, could be a part of the great Todd Freeman legacy of the Florida Keys?" He sent a positively religious gaze to the stars, his hands wide and splayed above his head.

Todd burst out laughing. "Sure, Davey. Why not?"

"What about your coin idea, mang?" Davis asked. He pulled out the very cart Todd thought he'd had his eye on, shaking it free in a jangle from the connecting fleet lined up against the outer wall of the building. "You find a weird one, or something?"

"As a matter of fact, I just found one today. It *is* kind of funny looking. I might use it before I call up any collectors to price it, I don't know. Maybe I'll do my own research first to see if I can get any ideas."

Davis rolled the cart past him and into the store, where Todd was already looking for the handcarts that he always found near the front by the newspaper stands.

"It's not a doubloon, is it?" Davis asked with raised eyebrows, carefully enunciating the word *doubloon*.

"Oh man, I wish! Mel Fisher, I am not."

"Before you do give it away or sell it, I wouldn't mind seeing it myself."

"What? The funny penny?"

Davis nodded. "Yeah. I'm curious."

Todd shrugged casually as they ventured deeper into the brightly lit store, past the produce section. "No prob. Fifteen minutes?"

"Back at the truck, baby." Davis threw a thumb behind his back and pushed his cart into the depths of the store while Todd strolled to the beer section.

*

The Winn-Dixie was unexpectedly quiet for a late summer night, but then again it was Thursday, and Thursdays were hardly ever crowded. Too, Todd chalked it up to the effects of the long Labor Day weekend that had just passed, to the memory of fighting one's way through a grocery store during a holiday.

They were in and out in the allotted fifteen minutes as planned, booze and groceries in tow. Davis had skimped on the regular supplies this week and when Todd pressed him about the meager haul on the way back to their respective homes (like Todd, Davis had a small apartment above his bar, making them more than just business neighbors), he said he was saving room in the fridge. He had just reserved three huge slabs of ribs for himself.

"It's why you caught me going to the store so late, too. I gotta guy there that works a later shift. He gave me a sweet deal on those baby backs." A call for a belated Labor Day weekend grill-out was in order and, of course, Todd was more than invited. "Maybe for once you can trade in that metal-detector for a fishing pole and catch us something good to eat, ya beach bum!" Davis quipped, which Todd actually thought might be a good idea.

After thanking Davis for the ride and gathering his grocery bag and frosty six-pack, Todd turned to head up the steps to his apartment. Davis called to him a final time, "Oh, and Todd?"

"Yeah, *mang*?" Todd called back with a little smile, his keys jingling in his hand.

"I wanna see that coin you found!" Davis tilted his head and pointed at him like a big brother reminding his younger sibling to wash up before mom got home.

"You got it! I'll show you tomorrow."

"Morning?"

"Uh…Sure!"

"You better! Night, man!" *Mang.*

"Have a good one, bud!" And with that, Davis and Todd shared a final wave for the night. The departing truck rattled off down the alley.

As Todd unlocked his door and made his way into the dim apartment, he had to kick himself for not prodding Davis further about bringing anything to his grill-out, beyond the ha-ha of catching some fish. Sure, Todd could've very easily texted Davis about it, but thought better of it, thinking he would just ask him tomorrow when he strolled into Southern Cross to show him the coin. He figured in the morning, since he seemed so eager to see it. If nothing else, it would give them something to chat about.

Unfortunately, and unbeknownst to Todd, of course, that night's final wave would signal the end of their relationship as they knew it. There would be no grill-out, and the next time the two men saw each other would be under very, very different circumstances.

CHAPTER 3

JARS

LESS THAN TWENTY minutes later, Todd Freeman sat at his desk, silhouetted by the window that overlooked the roof of Southern Cross and a section of its open-air porch, sipping a beer. Low hanging clouds drifted by like tired ghosts, dimly illuminated by the glow of the city.

He might have confessed to Davis the details of his plans to stay in tonight, but he failed to mention how much the overlapping, varied coin idea was actually beginning to burn a hole in his head the more he considered it. Realizing he would've probably come off as his own fanboy, he was glad he hadn't brought it up any more to Davis.

Scavenging had its advantages when it came to loose change. As he'd explained to Davis, he had three Mayonnaise jars full of coins: American, Cuban, Bahamian, and Jamaican all mixed together. Unfortunately, no doubloons just yet. These jars were usually filled in a considerably short timeframe, even more so during the busy seasons. At least twice every year, Todd went down to the bank and picked up a stack of the four coin wrappers for American quarters, dimes, nickels and pennies. Yes, he could have gone to those machines in the grocery store that paid you in paper money for your epic spare change dump, but he chose to go at it the old fashioned way, like he did with *The Citizen* when he found something worthwhile, or opting to stick with an old-school clamshell flip phone in a world of iPhones and bluetooths. Sometimes, the old-fashioned way was just better, fitting.

Then, during the evening, he would put on some soft tunes—acid jazz, usually—surf the Internet on his five year old Mac, find some nice shots of the Mexican coast or the different beaches of the Keys for mural ideas, down some nightcaps, and fill the wrapping papers with his found money. If done correctly, routine was therapeutic.

On most nights, Todd could pick up the jazz station out of Miami, and if not there, then the one out of Ft. Myers. If neither one worked—if a storm came through, say—then he could find one streaming on the web, or send some Bob Marley through the speakers. Currently, he listened to soft horns out of Miami as the station came in strong.

Opening his fanny pack in front of the computer and spilling the contents out on the desk, he eyed the easel in the corner of the open room where a black canvas of abstract floral awaited him and wondered if he could finish it by tomorrow afternoon for the weekend crowd. He thought he probably could.

On the desk a small mound of mostly pennies, a few nickels, a cute little shell that he wanted to draw, and a few tabs from soda cans (something he also saved for recycling purposes) spread out on the wood surface, with one single quarter falling to the floor.

And sand, of course. There was always sand.

Examining the array of his various finds, Todd was struck again, with the idea for his 'Equality' series, and not just the coins, but shells, or even coral. The possibilities were endless.

One thing at a time, Toddy. See if the coins even look good stacked on top of each like that first.

The scattering of pennies against the wooden desk could fill a canvas nicely, and with the moonlight and the white blush of the monitor, there was a cozy splash of a very relatable "end-of-a-long-day" feel. After all, everyone pulled out their change at the end of the day, right?

In recent weeks, he'd tinkered with the notion of curving the direction of his paintings away from just tropical and floral-themed pieces. He just didn't know where to start. Short-Term Artist's Block, you could say. This Equality idea, however, could be a nice jump off. He kept his digital camera near his printer for when inspiration struck and of course for high quality images for online sales. Taking a few shots of the scattering of coins in front of him at different angles, he thought it would be a nice distraction to have a bigger project for the coming months.

Not that the seasons brought great changes in the Keys, in temperature or tourists.

For Todd, autumn's arrival brought a darker significance. One he couldn't ignore, no matter how hard he tried. Having a project to anchor him would help, but he knew the pain was inevitable.

Carefully, and to distract himself from that storm swelling in his heart that almost reached his throat, he centered the camera, focused it, and captured the shots. The streetlamps outside, as well as the lighting from Southern Cross, cut shadows over the desk he found attractive and fitting for the mood he wanted to capture. The angle, emotion, and lighting that he saw in his mind that jazzed him up so on his bike ride from the beach.

Maybe one more... he thought.

Click.

It was then, through the camera's eye, he spotted the strange little coin he had found on the beach, the funny penny the likes of which he'd never seen before. The rust-colored disc of metal was centered amid the rest of the coinage, hiding under two old, tarnished Lincolns. It was essentially the same color as the others, yet once he saw it the coin stood out like a boil.

He picked it up, examined it by the light from the window, and felt that the coin, again, had some significant weight to it, *surprising* weight. Clicking on the long-necked lamp attached to the edge of his desk, he craned it into position over the coin, the white light softly humming.

The side with the male profile, he found, wore a Roman Centurion-style helmet, the kind from maybe the first century (or so Todd guessed, who was he to know?), complete with a fuzzy crest jutting from its crown.

Immediately, he thought: *Gotta be fake.*

Then, immediately following that: *Maybe it's not.*

Some part of him said it was a joke, a novelty, something you could buy at a comic book store or a toyshop. A bigger part of him said this was something grand.

Something real.

Engraved around the edge of the coin was writing that looked like a form of Grecian script, adding to the genuineness of it. Whether one word or individual symbols, Todd couldn't tell.

There were no words or even any pictures on the other side, just tiny, strangely curved, embossed lines. Under closer scrutiny, he found there was a small dot centered among the lines that could have been anything from a symbol to nothing more than a single letter. To him, under the magnifying glass, it only looked like an embossed dot.

After he pulled some rubbing alcohol out of his desk with a rag and cleaned the coin, he still thought that the weight of it was the chief clue to its authenticity. The cleaning did nothing to change the look or color of the coin, though the embossed lines and random dot didn't wash off.

Todd blinked. Todd scoffed. Presuming it was going to be nothing, hell, leaning *hard* that it was nothing, he remembered he wanted to email his contact, Alex, for any advice on his new find.

He knew it was hitting the Easy Button, but he also knew from experience Alex was always a reliable start.

Alex Washington was a coin expert who lived in Miami, to whom Todd had turned a few times with the small handful of peculiar or unfamiliar coins he had come across. Their relationship had started out simply enough: Todd found him on the web and emailed him the information he needed about a dime dating back to 1912. He had discovered the dime on the south end of Higgs Beach a couple of years back, after a sizable tropical storm struck the region. It wasn't worth as much as he would have liked, but it started a working relationship that had matured into an online friendship.

It was in this relationship he'd discovered another romantic quality to his daily scavenging: the mystery of the voyage. How in the world had something like that dime found its way all the way down here in the Keys after a hundred-plus years odyssey? How many pockets, cash registers, and hands had it known? For that matter, how long had it been in the ocean? How many fish did it see? How many shells did it brush against? The thought was mind-bogglingly infinite, and fascinated him to his core.

Of the little he knew of Alex Washington, one thing was clear: he was a transplant who loved Miami, and the state of Florida. It was peppered in his emails, gushing over the gorgeous southern sunshine, or an eye-popping sunset, and how lucky they were to be there. Alex had inherited his coin shop, the Five and Dime, from an uncle. It was a store that also brought in other accessories that would fit a man of style. Expensive custom-made lighters, cufflinks, watches, and other collector's items, that would be handsome additions to a tasteful man's garb, were just a few of the other select items now found at The Five and Dime, according to the low-maintenance website Todd had found. Those were just objects to lure people into the continued traditions of collecting stamps, baseball cards and, of course, coins from around the world.

Todd jumped on his computer and pulled up his email account, but not without noticing and two-finger kissing the school picture of the smiling little blonde boy taped to the upper right corner of the monitor. Then, he opened the mouth of his printer, scanning the coin on one side and then the other. The images popped up on his screen a few seconds later. He hoped he wouldn't look stupid to Alex, but if this coin were the real thing, if he had stumbled upon something of real value, Alex would surely know.

He wrote:

Subject: Another Inquiry

Alex!

I know its been a long time, please forgive me, my friend. I hope everything is well with you. In search of some advice with this coin I found. It looks authentic, *feels* authentic too, but I don't want to get my hopes up. I'm feeling lucky today (fingers are crossed). Tell me I won, man!

Regards

TF

PS - One of these days I'm gonna have to get your direct number so I can just text you these pictures instead! :^)

Outside, there was an earsplitting scream and a burst of jovial laughter. Todd leaned over his chair toward the window to watch a group of large women from Southern Cross leave to go about their evening, their cameras bouncing on their abundant bosoms.

Todd read the email over a couple of times, then attached the two newly scanned images. It usually took Alex anywhere from three days to a week to respond, so he'd have to file it in the back of his mind for now. He slid the coin with the funny little lines and the Roman soldier to the side of his desk but kept his eyes on it.

To the coin he muttered aloud, "Where would I even begin with you?"

Todd turned back to the white-glow of the monitor, to the email to Alex, and wondered what phrase or word he would even search online to get him started. Ancient coins? Ancient Roman coins? Ancient doubloons? Coins with funny lines? Funny pennies? All of them sounded so broad, not to mention incredibly unlikely to guide him, that Todd was struck with a touch of paralysis through analysis. Plus, he didn't need to get lost in a rabbit hole of online searching when he had an expert to ask at his fingertips (and a painting to finish across the room). It was sort of like when the detective called him about the Jeremy Patrick crowbar: he handed it over and Todd was just in for the ride after that. Art and Finding was his expertise, so let the expert do his part...

The Send button awaited him.

He cracked open another beer and hovered the mouse over the button.

Todd took a long swig, and hoped he didn't sound too green in his email.

Click.

His computer gave a *swooshing* noise as the email blasted off.

"Tell me I can retire, dude." He began searching for some images he might use in his new art series, chuckling that this *was* the retirement dream for most people. It was even his dream of retirement just a few years ago. Only Todd expected this part of his life to come around sixty, not in his forties. But with everything that had happened, if this was his fallout, no one would ever hear a single complaint from him.

He peered past the monitor to the canvas, and the line up of alcohol inks and paint pens—the itch needing a scratch. He adjusted the music to the Reggae channel on his streaming service, stood, touched the school picture taped to the monitor again, and said, "See ya later, Big Guy.

His paint session was a good one, satisfying, even. With three beers in, he nearly finished his latest canvas, a stunning, colorful, eye-popping piece that drifted toward full-on floral abstract. But his session was enough for him to sway to the tunes and scratch his itch.

For him, it was the perfect way to end his day.

Enjoy it, Selfless Scavenger, while you still can. You have a very long day ahead of you.

CHAPTER 4

SEASONS

EARLY AUTUMN WAS always the worst for Todd. A little over four years ago, Todd was a completely different person, one that any of his current friends wouldn't have recognized and, most likely, would have never believed existed; a person he could hardly recollect himself. He was a man that would have been known locally in Dayton, Ohio, not as an artist, but as a fair-weather political advocate and contracts manager in a company that dealt with government defense and space. Mostly defense.

Buried deep inside of Todd, there was a serious, professional artist hiding. Somewhere. Had anyone suggested this leading up to the end of his corporate career, though, he would have laughed, and anyone who knew him would have laughed with him.

Todd wasn't a complete stranger to creativity, though. He excelled in art class and composition during his high school years and even in early college. Before he entered the political and military environment of defense contracting—discovering the kind of positions and the kind of money and personal security that was a real possibility in that industry—he found work as a draftsman and made good at it. It was during that time as a draftsman, while in college at Miami University in Oxford, Ohio, that he'd met his wife-to-be, Emma Ross. It was his budding skills with a pencil, pen, and paintbrush that attracted her to him, and Todd knew it. It was his passion and drive for what he did and what he loved, his confidence and his security that his art was the most honest thing he could ever do. It was what made her fall in love with him. It was his creative, right-side-of-the-brain outlook. It was the way he could create anything he wanted to on a blank canvas and form it into something of complete beauty and radiance: a landscape, a courtyard, a butterfly, a portrait of Emma, it didn't matter. Todd could draw it.

Todd found a muse in Emma too, as well as a fiery love that he had never experienced before with any other woman. Her own passion for life and her unique and colorful vibrancy, not to mention her razor sharp sense of humor that brought Todd to tears of laughter over three dozen times in just the first year of dating, drove his work and his growing love for her.

Meanwhile, the wheels were vigorously turning for Todd to be living the All-American Dream when he landed his solid, well-paying job in government contracting before even graduating college, rocketing him toward middle management in a few short years. A new, different kind of security beyond the honesty of his creativity and artwork was offered, one geared more toward financial and employment security that comes with a full-time career. The road to the Dream he was raised to desire was paved before his eyes. The three-bedroom house, the stable job with the 401k and stock options, the two cars and a safe neighborhood that brought with it one of the best schools in the state, would come easily afterward, as would retirement and barbecues on the weekends.

Early on in their marriage, when he wasn't putting in the overtime or washing the car or some other mundane chore that came with his post as a husband, he gradually converted the garage into the studio of his own personal, artistic dreams. Emma was all for it, even if there were mounds of snow in the mornings when she needed to clean off her windshield and there wasn't enough room for the second car. A year after starting the project, and only two years after settling into the house just inside the city limits of Centerville—a humble suburb of Dayton—the studio was finally complete, along with heating, central air, and clean, clear lighting for his portraits and canvases.

Only, it was around the same time that, after just two years, more responsibility, and countless hours of overtime, his company couldn't deny the influence Todd had on the performance and integrity of his coworkers, not to mention the soaring profits the company was experiencing. It seemed he had as much a knack for contracting as art. They handed him a major promotion and an even higher position, allowing him to catch up on the never-ending bills and even bonus pay for the diapers for his newborn son, Kyle.

Once all that happened, the believed-to-be All-American Dream, like moss creeping over a fallen tree, began to overtake Todd's personal aspirations for his art. The paint and canvases were shoved aside to make room for the mini-van in the garage for Emma and Kyle during those cold Ohio days that seemed to slip from grey skies to black within mere hours.

Pressure built, as did the hours in the office and the expectations that followed. Like his superiors before him, Todd's belly grew and the bags under his eyes became heavier, the wrinkles carved deeper into the edges of his eyes and extending into his temples. Soon enough, sleep eluded him, and the headaches of the job were coming in faster and harder than he would have liked.

Kyle grew, mortgage payments were paid, years blew by like pages against the wind, and Todd's paintings and art aspirations went beyond the back burner and into the corner of the furnace. The garage needed to be cleaned to make room for the luxury sports car both he and Emma had lusted after for years. In the long run, they both knew it had only been another distraction from what both of them really wanted, what they had come into this marriage for in the first place—time together, something there was less and less of over the years.

Prisoner, thy name is Freeman. Oh, the irony.

Collecting dust, his easel cracked and fell apart. Without notice, bugs and mice picked to pieces the brushes for their nests while the paint turned and had to be thrown out. The canvases were degraded and Todd's desire all but died the day the tools he loved so dearly so long ago sat at the end of the driveway, awaiting the trash-man.

Yes, the Freeman family was doing quite well for themselves, especially for their age. Especially for the economy. *Booming,* even, as one relative had once pointed out at one of Kyle's early double-digit birthday parties. And while a select few of Todd's finest works hung in the hallways and bedrooms throughout the house as a constant reminder of Todd's talented college days, when the courage and the passion burned in a way only younger men knew, Todd never felt the desire to return to that stage of his life. All of it quietly became part of the background, a silly delusion of the past and of a young man who needed to 'get with the program' and 'get a real job.'

"I noticed one of your little doodles on your notes from our last meeting, Todd," said one of his older superiors, once. "What are those?"

The older man, a cranky stiff with liver spots on his hands and a tendency for violence toward technology he didn't understand, had been seated in his office when he posed that question, Todd seated across from him. "Oh, those?" Todd said, glancing at the notepad in his hand.

"Yes. So...what? Are you an artist or something?"

"I was," Todd said, and even as the words left his mouth, he cringed a little. It felt like he had just spat in the face of a dear friend, so he corrected himself. "I-I mean, I am."

"Why? Why do you do it? You don't think you could do anything with that, do you? Anything *meaningful*, anyway? You know all those artist types are nothing but a bunch of timewasters. Heathens, if you ask me." He waved his wrinkled claw-hand in the air with a dismissive fat lip stuck out, even though his lips were anything but. Added to this were short, dismissive shakes of his nearly hairless head. "Good to know that a young man like yourself finally got with the program and dismissed all those juvenile things. All those bottom-feeding bums need to get a real job. You got your career and your child to think about."

Get with the program. Get a real job.

The colors and the canvases were just…there…now, because he had needed to get with the program. He had needed a real job.

Yes, during his time with the company, Todd was known in his office in Dayton as the free-spirited manager (something the old-codger frowned upon during his whole tenure there); a manager who doodled on his inner-office memos to earn a smile from someone and had even done little cartoons of different coworkers on his marker board. Though, nothing more serious than that. But after enough time, his reputation as an inner-office doodle artist quickly began to shed like a skin as well. He knew that was a good thing too. He didn't want to push the envelope of the company's high standards of professionalism, or its strict conservative culture.

All the same, when some offices are fortunate enough to have a boss like Todd, they don't know what they have until it's gone. As he continued to move into higher positions, taking on more responsibilities over the years, general morale in the company burned brighter, and former coworkers who'd had the privilege to work under him in the past reminded him of that almost daily in the halls, or in passing conversation in the restrooms.

By the time Todd was running his own division in the company—and a big one at that—Kyle was a growing, young man, influenced by his father's important work with defense missiles and big rockets and aircraft fighters and bombers. He started playing more war themed video games, haunting gun ranges, watching more military based films, reading Tom Clancy almost exclusively.

Soon, Kyle was talking of going to fight against ISIS and ISIL, in Afghanistan, Iraq, and throughout the Middle East and Syria if he needed to, fighting terrorism and protecting the country he loved. Todd *did* swell with pride for his son, but certainly not without a heavy and considerable degree of worry. He spoke of him to his coworkers not as a boy of late seventeen, but as a man who wanted to fight for what was right in his brave heart. Still, in the back of his mind, there was that lurking fear that Kyle wouldn't come back. That he would be one of those victims in a Breaking News report on CNN or Fox News, having been captured and tortured for information or killed in an attack on a moving caravan. Or maybe even in friendly fire. What if he was permanently injured? Or he lost a limb? What if he came back in a box?

Eventually, as time ticked on and Kyle's eighteenth birthday drew closer, Emma became more and more distressed over her son's coming decision of joining the war. She didn't want him to go and pleaded with Todd to convince him to go another route. Notably college.

"I want this, dad," Kyle had said, sitting at the edge of the lake in Hueston Woods with a fishing pole and a limp wire hanging from the end. "It would make everyone proud. I know it would."

"We're *already* proud of you, son. But your mother is incredibly worried. You know that, right?"

"I know," he said. Todd didn't think he was going to go on. His son was watching the still water, looking for fish. "I know she is. But I have to do what's right, and I know this is."

The seasons changed and as quickly as the temperature dropped, the call came, the one both he and Emma had been dreading, but Kyle had been aching over. The United States Army had welcomed him aboard. And suddenly, the house was empty. Their son had gone to the other side of the world to fight.

Everyday, Todd would ask Emma if she heard anything from him, especially the first few weeks. While the letters and calls were sparse, Kyle sounded happy and enthusiastic in the training academy. That was what mattered, but Emma still worried. Honestly, so did Todd. His wife would slip into periods of depression where she couldn't sleep, and Todd didn't have to ask to know what was wrong.

At his work, however, the climate was very different. The attitude was the polar opposite, in fact. A smile and a proud clap on the back would accompany the inquiries of his son, which would happen nearly every day from different people as a reminder that he wasn't a little boy anymore. He wasn't at home waiting on him on the steps of the porch, waiting for dad, waiting for him to show up so he could run and jump into his embrace and throw his skinny little arms around his neck at his father's arrival. He wasn't at the canvas either, painting his little picture that Todd would then hang in his office with pride; more pride than any random fighter jet or degree could have ever given him.

No, little Kyle was on the other side of the globe, living in tents and in the mountains, surrounded by enemies.

All of this went on for about thirty months or so. The rare-but-steady calls and letters never stopped, as did Emma's depression and his coworkers' questions.

The one thing that *did* change was the mood of the letters and the sound of their son's voice during his calls, few and far between that they were. There wasn't that excitement and that thrill anymore. In one letter, he admitted he sometimes wondered if this was what he truly wanted. Saying he missed them came more often too, but he never once made mention that his decision was a mistake. He faltered, but held steady to his choice. And for that, Todd and Emma would be proud of him forever.

Then, one day, the nightmare came true.

Kids selling cable subscriptions, girl scouts, and Jehovah's Witnesses would come to their house at times, sending Todd or Emma to the front door with a nervous, trembling hand. Images of the military messenger, sporting the uniform with his cap held humbly in his hand, would immediately spring to mind, but when they saw the visitors only wanted to sell cookies or a subscription to a new cable provider, their hearts fluttering, their breath baited, they happily declined, relieved beyond description. After the door was shut and that awkward, but eternally relieved, moment between them would pass—always with a knowing glance at each other as to what that call *could* have been—they would go on with their evening affairs in that haunting disquiet, never broaching the topic.

So, when the representative of the army corps stood at their doorstep one rainy, cold day in late November, after the sun had set at an outrageous time of 5:30 in the evening, tears were already pooling in their eyes before the young man even spoke. Todd tried to stay calm. He tried to hold it back as best he could, clinging to Emma as she clung to him. Distantly, he could feel the wetness of her tears already soaking through his shirt, just below his shoulder. He could also feel his bottom lip start to tremble uncontrollably, his voice wilting in his throat.

It was like in a made-for-TV movie, everything in slow motion and liquidy around the edges. The look in the young man's eyes said it all. It wasn't until the stoic representative gave them the news in actual words out loud that Todd broke down and began clutching the wall for balance, slipping away from Emma's grip and his composure. Emma's face had transformed into a warped grimace, as her hand covered her mouth against the tiny, throaty squeak escaping her. Todd's lips, well past the trembling stage and fully quaking by then, pulled back in overwhelming grief to show teeth. After that, his knees gave out, all energy in his body howling from his lungs. Somewhere in another time zone, Emma produced one more voiceless, choking peep. Then the screams erupted from her, too.

Only one thought blazed in his mind as Todd fell to the floor: five-year-old Kyle sitting on the stool at his own miniature easel, next to Todd's own. In his son's small, chubby hand was a little paintbrush being waved about like it was a magic wand, laughing at the colors on the canvas, looking up at his dad as giggles echoed in the garage. That day they had painted for three hours together. Todd couldn't get into his own groove that morning until little Kyle had peeked in, seeing the annoyance on his father's face from the doorway. Quietly, he had joined him at his own miniature easel, just to the right of his Pop's. Before they knew it, they were laughing and talking and merely enjoying themselves. Father and son, having a ball together, making silly pictures they would later hang.

"Daddy," Kyle had said, once the brushes were cleaned and dinner was calling them, "this is the best day of my whole life."

Todd had chuckled, rubbed the top of his son's head, and admitted to him, "This is the best day of *my* whole life too, son."

For Todd, time had stopped at that memory.

Kyle had been killed in a Taliban bombing outside the village he had talked about in his last contact with them, just three weeks before. After Todd collapsed against the wall and onto the floor, he began to shake. His whole person. His face grew hot. He could feel it: he was losing control. His entire body felt like he was going to explode.

On the floor, he covered his mouth with his hands and wept with his wife as she joined him there, pulling each other close to the point of almost tumbling over together onto the porch. The young army representative bent to help, but Todd pushed him away, hating the uniformed man for touching him.

The young soldier, who looked around thirty and far more muscular than Todd had ever been in his entire life, understood the overwhelming grief and backed away from Todd and Emma, giving them space.

After the young man left, and the long, long night began, something changed in Todd.

He didn't sleep that night, spending most of the darkest hours in solitude in his upstairs office chair with a roll of toilet paper, staring out at the stars. Sometime around four in the morning, right after Emma had lost her voice from crying and screaming with her own piles of balled-up Kleenex scattered throughout their bedroom, she had drained herself of energy and had fallen asleep. With that, Todd felt a shred of gratitude. He needed to be alone. He needed the silence.

After he escaped into his office, he actually considered, for three grueling hours in the weak morning light, where frost covered most of the lower half of the window and slowly skated up the glass, that he would kill himself, right there, right then. He owned a gun and knew it wouldn't be that hard. The pain was immense. And it was because of Todd's career, *his* influence, that his only son was dead. The blame was his. The planes, the rockets, the ships had all struck an unexpected chord in their little boy...

Eventually...*eventually*...Todd decided against suicide. He didn't know why he didn't do it then. During the eventual long, exhausting therapy sessions, when he felt awkward, depressed, drained and miserable, he wondered, again, why he hadn't gone through with it. Why he hadn't just tasted the cold metal at his lips. When he and Emma began to sour, he thought again about why he didn't take the gun, shove it in his mouth, and pull the damn trigger that first night. He thought about it when he finally returned to the office, weeks later and almost fifteen pounds lighter, thinking he needed to escape into his work.

Finish this non-disclosure agreement. Be on this team for this exciting new project with this new customer! Did you get the point of contact for that one subcontractor in San Diego? Could you handle the HR girl who isn't getting along with your new temp?

And so on and so on and so on…

The drum forever beating.

Todd barely heard the sound.

CHAPTER 5

SEASONS CHANGE

EMMA LEFT A year later. There was no getting around that. The papers from her lawyer came within the month of her departure, as was expected. She wanted that part of her life to be done. *She* was done. And honestly, so was he.

They sold the house and split the winnings, or losses, depending on how you saw it. The cars were split as well. She got the Mercedes, he got the Viper. Todd notified the company that things weren't going in the direction he would've liked and promptly submitted his two-week notice.

Todd scheduled a meeting with the heads of HR, one of the last he would ever attend, and decided to take his severance package early, cashing in his decently-sized 401k and adding up the earnings from his stocks—all this against his broker's wide-eyed admonition. But it didn't matter, since he figured it was enough funds to get him far, far away from Dayton, Ohio.

This part of Todd's life was over. Call it a mid-life crisis, or call it the turning of a page, a new chapter in his journey, renewal, growth. Todd didn't care what one might call it. He just knew the money would get him to a warmer climate, away from the changing seasons and the falling leaves and cold, snowy nights where frost bit at the bottoms of windows and skated up the glass, like it did the night he should have ended it all. Away from the reminders of what was and what could have been.

Todd Freeman didn't know where his life was headed, but he knew he had to be brave to find out. He *needed* to find out what was beyond this bitter and abysmally sad stage and to get out of the environment he was in, to start anew with his past and former life held close to his heart. He didn't know if he would be able to do that if he remained in Ohio; he really didn't. The memories were everywhere. The nostalgia was overbearing most days.

He didn't know where his actions were taking him when he traded in the Dodge Viper for straight cash and purchased a scratched, dented, and completely ancient Buick Roadmaster station wagon, either. Old as hell, but cheap as hell too, and with low, low miles.

Sold.

Late the follow week, just before sunrise, he drove through the dark streets of Miamisburg, a small southern suburb of Dayton, to the southbound exit of Interstate-75 for a final time. He had avoided the Christmas traffic of the Dayton Mall by a wide berth of time, making sure nothing was going to slow him down. Only two duffle bags were in the back seat of the Buick that cold morning: one filled with clothes, the other with pictures and video of Kyle.

That was it. Everything else was sold and gone. His career, his car, his home, his wife and mother of his child, his whole life, and everything else in between, were all behind him now. Call it a transition if you wanted to, a shedding, a metamorphosis, or a rebirth. Todd began to like the sound of all four because each of them felt...*right*.

And as he crossed over the Ohio River into Covington, Cincinnati's impressive skyline behind him and the first waves of Northern Kentucky's rolling hills on the dim morning horizon, it just kept feeling right. Southwest Ohio was home to many good memories of his childhood, most of his adulthood, nearly his whole life. So, it was heartbreaking to see it all recede behind him. He wondered when he was going to see it again, or if he ever would.

It was just after seven o'clock when he crossed over that natural border of the Ohio River into Kentucky, when the sun was peeking over the bluegrass valleys, hiding its saffron glow behind the hills and the trees, reflecting cold light onto the frigid looking skyscrapers. Cincinnati looked magical. The cloudless sky, the white, snow-covered tops of the buildings and the dulled tones of the sunlight made it look like a fictional city, like Oz or Metropolis. Goodbye, old friend.

*

He drove all day.

Kentucky and Tennessee flew by in a fog as thick as the mists hanging over the Smoky Mountains. His brain and body were cruising on automatic, driving the behemoth of a car down the freeway, every emotion he could conjure touching upon him during the trip. It wasn't until he reached the Florida-Georgia border the next day—after fighting a huge traffic jam south of Knoxville, a late night conversation about road trips with a young black waitress with two kids in an Atlanta Denny's, and a close call with a highway patrolman near Macon—that his running thoughts finally arrived at painting and art. It was, admittedly, the first time he had thought about it in a very long time.

But with that passing thought, a walk-on cameo and nothing more, a subtle and forgotten comfort crept into his heart. It was like hearing a song he hadn't heard in years. Or smelling an aroma that triggers the memory banks of good times.

He drove on.

Because it was late December, only a few days from the second Christmas without his son alive, and the first without his wife with him, the weather was encouragingly temperate at the border. Low sixties, average humidity with mostly cloudy skies. A sprinkling of palm trees welcomed him into Florida, the first he'd seen.

Still, it was too close for him.

He drove on.

When he reached the northern tip of the Florida Turnpike that could lead him to Orlando and other happy families ready to see Mickey Mouse, he inadvertently pressed a little harder on the gas petal. He sped past the onramp, choosing to go through Tampa, Sarasota, and the Gulf Coast instead.

Given, Todd wasn't completely optimistic about this trip south and really didn't know where this whole experiment was taking him. Yeah, he thought a place down here would be good for him, but after that…what? Sell oranges on the side of the road? Take up surfing? Quitting a good job, settling for a mutual divorce without much fight, and selling your home of well over fifteen years to pick up and move to another state were all major, not to mention majorly traumatic, things to do in a such a short time. In fact, he wondered what force, beyond his personal grief and desire for warmer temperatures, was pulling him down here. *Was it to start a new life? To get away from the past?*

To try and forget about everything, like Emma wanted to?

No.

He hadn't the slightest clue where he was going or what he was going to do when he got there, but he knew for a fact that he wasn't going to forget. That's what the duffle bag full of pictures was for. The photos in the bag were mainly of Kyle, but there were some of Emma as well, cherished moments that kept his love for her alive deep within him; an appreciation for their adventure together. Keeping friends with your ghosts makes them not jump out and scare you as much.

Passing Sarasota, seeing signs for the Cultured Coast and a billboard featuring the art institute (which gave his heart another queer little tickle in its own right), he still continued driving. He skirted Fort Myers, even though the climate had improved and transformed into what he was searching for—sky that had a striking glow to it as bright as the sun, and more palm trees than he could count.

Yet, he drove on.

He reached Naples and sidestepped the city, going across the Alligator Alley of Interstate-75, speeding through that highway's home stretch before meeting up with I-95.

At the outskirts of Fort Lauderdale, he arrived at the Gold Coast of South Florida on an eighth of a tank.

*

While pumping gas at a station in the adorable little community of Weston, Florida, Todd heard the radio in a young man's convertible blasting some loud hip-hop music. The DJ eventually came on with her overly enthusiastic voice, stating that the temperature was a balmy 78 degrees in the city, and that the poor folks up north were experiencing record low temperatures. *My goodness, how lucky we are, yo,* said the hyped voice on the radio. The DJ never stated a particular city, but Todd had an inkling that Dayton and Cincinnati were somewhere in the mix of those record numbers. Ohio usually was, when it came to low temperatures.

After pumping his tank full of unleaded, he spotted a sign in the distance leading to Interstate-95 South: a little less than two hundred miles to a place called Key West.

Key. West.

Todd thought there was a possibility of magic in such a name. A name he had of course heard of, but hadn't really considered until that moment. Hadn't even been on his radar, in fact.

He drove on.

As he merged off I-95 and onto the US 1 South to the Keys, going into the busy stretch of land through Key Largo and finding the road and the area becoming increasingly vacant of people, he was overwhelmed with the deep sense that he was driving into another world—a secret world—one that somehow was cut off from the rest of society; one that hardly concerned itself with the rest of the country. He couldn't help being reminded of the feeling he'd had not even a few days before when he left Ohio for his own grand mystery ahead. If leaving Dayton behind and crossing over the Ohio River were his own spiritual contractions and mental dilations in this emotional delivery, then this, right here, was the actual rebirth.

Become anew, Todd Freeman, fresh and sacred in these warm, tropical waters.

Shed and become reborn.

This is a beginning.

Soon enough, water replaced land all around him. Exotically-named towns and tiny islands whizzed past him in a floral, island-hopping blur. Some were so small they contained only small pockets of recognizable civilization. A bank here…a fishing market there…scattered fragments of life spread across a warm and sprawling aquatic blanket of tranquility.

How do these people live down here? Where's the grocery store to buy food and beer and Ambisol? Where do they get haircuts? Where do they buy their shoes? Todd started to worry, wondering if he'd dropped over the edge of the culture, so to speak, moving into some kind of neither-region.

But then, about halfway through the long stretch to Key West, right around the time he passed the tiny blip of a town that was Layton, Florida, a funny thing started to happen to him. A lucid, inner wave of relaxation like he had never experienced swept over him. He could almost see the clouds of stress and bad energy leaving his pores, like black steam evaporating off hot coals, to blow out the driver's side window and be taken by the ocean air.

On the radio station he picked up, the music was soft and relaxing, but also *groovable*, stirring in him a desire to dance. Even sing!

It was then he realized two things: the first was that the views of the Caribbean Sea, and the swell of clouds over the Gulf Stream, were *exactly* what he had been looking for.

The second was more of a feeling than a realization, an emotion he hoped to never forget: that this was his reward for his courage. For going on. For continuing.

For the first time in over two years, Todd felt…good. He spotted palm trees, and seaplanes, and smiling people, and boats galore. So many boats! All of them quietly riding the waves. Holding back tears, he wondered what Kyle would have thought of all the boats.

It was a little after five in the evening when he approached the outskirts of Key West, the Conch Republic as it was once called for a very short time, and Todd was greeted to the final island by one of the most stunning, breathtaking, and majestic sunsets he ever witnessed. As the sun inched closer to the crest of the horizon, an incredible thing began to happen around him—people were standing motionless on the banks of the little islands and the different bridges he was crossing.

They were simply standing there. Clusters of people, groups, couples, and individuals alike.

This, of course, struck Todd the Northerner as incredibly strange. Some folks were alone and others with their mates, arm and arm, hand in hand, as it finally dawned on Todd what they were doing—they were enjoying the sunset.

They were taking pause from their day just to enjoy the sunset. And as the last sliver of sun dipped below the ocean, Todd let a few tears escape when all the people applauded the sun's climax, and then went about their evening.

And he thought, for the first of many times that following week: *I may be on to something here.*

Something Found: A Coin

*

Todd bummed around the island for a few days, staying at a charming little hotel and taking in the floral scenery, the local culture, the dive bars, and the warm beaches at sunset. He rode down Duval Street in his old, beat up car like it was the Vegas Strip come early evening, drinking in the bubbly vibe of this tiny island city.

My God, he thought, surveying the variety of people moseying down the street, laughing, talking, smiling. *The energy of this place is bottomless! The creative energy, the positive energy! Why on earth haven't I been here before?*

And Todd thought, *Because it wasn't the right time yet. That's why.*

And for some reason, this gave him chills, but they were the good kind of chills. The kind you get when you know you've stumbled upon something grand and pure and absolutely right that has called upon you like a shining oracle. The human experience doesn't offer up that feeling very often, so Todd knew to cherish it when it came. In fact, he relished in it. Driving through the crowded, tropical streets where bongo music filled the air and palm trees swayed like something out of a fantasy, Todd, for first time in God knew how long, wasn't thinking about the past, but the future.

Briefly, he measured if this amped-up environment might be too much for a man his age, if there was too much energy and vivaciousness for a small-town Ohio boy like himself. Granted, he wasn't a crotchety old bird, but he was no spring chicken either. Judging by the cross-dressing clubs and scantily-clad women walking the streets, this place was in continual party mode.

Yet there was a certain comfort knowing this community was awake at three in the morning, enjoying the clement night, drinking, talking, laughing, creating, and most of all, *living*. They were *alive* and he wasn't alone.

He wasn't goddamn *alone*.

During the first week, Todd dropped by the Hemingway House, rode the tour trolley of the city, and went to the Southern Most Point in the entire country—gifting himself a personal tour and overview of this new and captivating island he never really knew existed at the literal end of the road.

On the second day of his second week in town, he went to the bank and checked on his funds—a little over three-hundred-and-fifty-thousand dollars sat there, stewing in its juices. Plenty to start over. Now the question was, *how?*

Todd had struck up a few conversations with other artists he'd met around town. All of them openly welcomed him to their community of painters, writers, and sculptors, showing a real, genuine interest in him and his arrival. He hoped he could truly be one of them one day as a plan began to form.

Something told him it wouldn't be very hard to pick up that brush again. He had been thinking about it more and more ever since he came to Florida, and after a few days in the Keys found he was aching—actually *aching*—for the brush in his hand and the stroke against the canvas.

He hoped it would come back to him like riding a bike, and he strongly believed it would. The one passion he had disregarded so long ago would *have* to come back to him, *must* come back to him, if he wanted to survive.

So, it was on the final day of the year that he set everything in motion. He found a small building nestled between a gift shop and a floral depot with a sign in the window advertising a large, spacious open downstairs studio and an unfurnished upstairs apartment, begging to be plucked from the market. The sign on the window even read: *A Creative Person's Nesting Ground.*

Sold.

Something Found: A Coin

*

Todd laid low his first couple of months in Key West. In an attempt to clear his mind and heart of the most hellish year of his life, and to reinstitute some kind of stability for his wavering sanity, he would stop by the beach to reflect as a cheap but effective kind of personal therapy. He strolled the shores with his heart in his hands, attempting to enjoy the uniqueness of the Sunset Celebrations, the calming serenity of the kite flyers, and finding comfort and inspiration in the sights and the people around town. Effortlessly, they would strike up overly zealous conversations with him, the friendly visitors sharing some heartwarming laughs, riding that sweet vacation high, or locals sharing some hilarious fishing or boating story.

Todd would always consent to these pleasant little exchanges. It was in his nature to. With that unexpected friendliness reaching out to him so effortlessly, the introverted slump Todd was in slowly began to reverse, like a sock being pulled right side out. Todd had inserted himself into a new city where nobody knew him and it was a strange mixture of sadness, freedom, and a touch of loneliness, so these interactions were welcomed extra warmly. Encouraged, uplifted, and thankful after these short but friendly chats, Todd felt the force of the city enfolding him, kneading him into the island's flow and character, cautiously accepting him as one of its own. These short little conversations were just tests, the Keys feeling him out, getting to know him. Todd had accepted the city. Now, would the city accept him?

Without a doubt, Todd's travels to the beach expanded his soul. Watching the waves, he was struck by the revelation that the tide line was, in fact, also a timeline.

Once it struck, he quickly embraced this undeniably uninspired model of the ocean and shore as a timeless blanket of infinity. Yet, the aquatic analogy of time and sea came to him quite often during his visits to Higgs, Smathers, and Ft. Zach Beach, more than he would have expected once the trips became routine. The way Todd saw it wasn't along the sandy coastline, the way some would naturally picture time stretching on into oblivion, but *outward*, starting at the dunes and spreading out toward the far-gone sea horizon.

Essentially, if the beach were the past, with its billions of grains of sand being the trillions of memories and experiences all connecting us, then the tide, slipping in and out, ebbing and flowing in our lives, was the present. The Current. The waves, either crashing or shuffling to the shore, were the Right Here And Now fluctuations of human life—the ups and the downs, the joys and the sorrows, the excitement and the boredom. It's a current we are all experiencing, even if it drifts by us entirely unnoticed in the background of the ocean's crests and downfalls. But it could also go undetected if we are still in the past, remaining on the beach, staying with the memories and not creating new ones to keep our toes warm when we eventually come back to visit them.

Todd became aware during his recurring visits to the beach that his eyes were drawn more to that ocean surface and the horizon beyond, well past the waves and the tide, to that calm Unknown Future waiting to become a crashing Right Here And Now. Looking upon the still face of the ocean to the horizon—his eyes so far away—Todd could only think of three little words: let's jump in.

*

With his still-tattered and still-healing emotions under control from a month of regular visits to the peaceful sands, Todd finally spent the money he had brought with him on two things he yearned for and needed, aside from the studio-apartment and its basic amenities, of course. Said purchases were something he needed for his famished soul; what the tranquil waters had coerced out of him to fill that sad vacancy in his broken heart.

Naturally, the first one was an easel—a nice strong one with sturdy legs.

He wouldn't be able to get the paint and brushes in his car just yet, being that it was packed with bedding and extras to decorate his new apartment, spoils from a full day of plundering at the local home furnishing store. Although, Todd had already picked out the different colors to slap on the canvas and even had a few other specialty art supplies on back order. In fact, he had spent more time at the paint store for canvas colors than on interior schemes for his new home. Still, at least with the easel, he was well on his way to what was calling back to him. He had a foundation to remind him of what was important now and how he needed to heal.

The second purchase was, of all things, a metal detector—a Matrix M6 model.

While he was there at the beach, sipping his beer in the afternoon shade of a swaying palm tree, he would watch, intrigued, as the guys with metal detectors all went about looking for something buried under the sand. A treasure left behind long ago, among the billions of memories and granules—something released by Mother Ocean, or some unsuspecting beachgoer's pocket. They were all...looking.

They were a unique group to him, for sure. That was obvious from the first time he saw them. Their absurdly large headphones, attached to the swaying device in a looping, spiraling cord which dangled around their arms and bumped against the sifter that hung from their belt like a gunslinger's holster, was all rather ridiculous to him. Although, there was a definite Floridian charm to their appearance he couldn't deny—the loose linen and shameless Hawaiian shirts, the flip-flops, the scratched shades they wore, their healthy bronzed skin. For the men, the scruffy sun-soaked five o'clock shadow. For the women, the glimmer of their chapstick-slathered lips reflecting in the sun. All of it together made up their optimistic, but odd, uniform they shared.

They're all looking for something found. Every one of them.

The grammar of the thought was wrong to him. He didn't know why, being that he wasn't a writer. It just was. It sounded… off. But like the move, the studio, and the courage to pick up the paintbrush again after such a wide gap of lost and painful time, it also sounded *right*. It sounded oh, so right.

Todd surveyed something peculiar about them, their crew, their clan, their dune-scavenging tribe. They always strode with their heads down, like monks in deep prayer. Completely at peace with themselves and knowing they were on a hunt, doing what they loved in their free time.

But none of that was what *lured* Todd to the idea of spending his time with a machine on a beach. The thing that fascinated Todd the most was when they looked up from the sand, distracted from the concentration of the search, and their eyes appeared so far away. Blissfully far.

That was what Todd found most attractive and eccentric: they were in another place, deep within themselves. They had tapped into some harmonic reservoir, swimming through soulwaters, seeking a hopeful sparkle. You couldn't find something like that working on a million-dollar contract with the local Air Force Base. Hell, Todd thought, you couldn't find that kind of peace working on a canvas. They were quietly content in their own little world, thinking, searching, and discovering more than just what was at their feet, but what was in their heads and hearts, waiting to be harvested from their memories among all that sand.

What Todd didn't know was that some folks already saw that quality in him when he looked to the horizon, the future, and the beyond.

With the detector in hand as he reached the sand that first

time, he knew he had already been bitten by the proverbial bug that so many scavengers spoke of when talking of their hunts. Honestly, *bitten* was probably too weak of a word. He had been gnawed at, tenderized and practically digested by that little guy.

It took two days and over six hours before he turned up a single thing—a dime from 1994 that looked about a hundred years older. Todd knew it was a small find, but it elated him nonetheless. After dusting off the sand and examining the dull coin, the first of many he would discover, he held it in front of his face and made the expression of a man learning an interesting fact. He pocketed the dime, and, when he got home, finished the mayonnaise jar with a turkey club on toasted white, cleaned the glass jar, and popped the dime into it.

Plink! The jar collection had started.

Todd didn't find anything of real value until two months and three beaches later, and it was a *whopper*. By the time he found that first ring, he had collected close to five dollars in extra change and had established his favorite beaches to go to, along with his least favorite. He couldn't believe he had found what he did—at Smathers Beach on a random Tuesday evening—but when he had stumbled across a silver band with the inscription of H & A '02 inside the loop, he felt terrible for the person, or rather, *couple*, who had lost it. Todd could only imagine the kind of distress and anguish the person who lost the ring must have been going through.

And it was in that moment he made the direct connection to his son, Kyle.

It was also in that moment he came to a profound personal realization. He understood why he wanted to go searching so passionately, why he felt so excited about having a simple tool to find things under the sand. It was because of his son. It was because he wanted a similar tool to find his son.

This immediately led Todd to consider what he could do to

help the owner of the lost ring, to bring them some relief. If there was any way he could bring it back to them.

These islands are getting to me if I'm becoming that generous, he thought later that evening, sitting on his second-hand couch and examining the ring. *What happened to finder's keepers, Todd?* Holding it up in the dwindling sunlight, he still couldn't believe he'd found it, let alone seriously consider trying to find the owner to return it to them. Todd had no idea what kind of herculean effort that would take.

Todd Freeman had come to a crossroads at that moment in his life that not many of us are blessed with. He was given a choice: keep the ring and sell it, or go the road less traveled, the road that led to him transforming into something that is on the endangered species list in this world: a good, bighearted person. There would be work involved in earning such a title, but it didn't take very long at all for Todd to know his answer.

The next morning he called up *The Citizen* newspaper and reported the lost ring. After that, he visited Craigslist, and a local version of that online classified site specifically aimed at the residents of the Keys, and submitted an ad to both of them. He didn't know what to expect, but he knew there were going to be swindlers who were going to try and swipe it out from under him, to try and play him for a fool with crocodile tears. Obviously, though, the partner would have the matching ring, which would help his situation tremendously.

It wasn't but a few days later that a man called him up at his studio claiming he had lost his ring and that it was an absolute miracle it was found. His name was Addison Hartley. He and his longtime boyfriend Harris had come down to the Keys on a lovely anniversary trip from Jacksonville to indulge in Key West's thriving and legendary gay community. Over the phone, he explained to Todd how they had already left the islands on a time constraint to return home, so it would have been a waste to go all the way back to Key West since, up until then, they had no idea where the lost ring could have gone. They had all but accepted that the ring had been found and was most likely pawned off for couple of bucks.

Gushing over the phone, Addison explained that most of their vacation had been riddled with grief and worry since they spent most of their time playing amateur gumshoes by revisiting the same places and retracing their steps. As Harris drove around the city in hopes of cheering up Addison's blues, Addison had been watching the postings through his smart phone the whole weekend with dwindling hope. It wasn't until they were 30 miles from home, way up in J-ville, that he caught Todd's posting.

He sent pictures of the match to Todd's email and proved that it was their ring. The style matched. The engravings matched. The font matched. The year matched. Todd was convinced. The next day he sent the ring first class priority mail. When he said he would return it, Addison was near tears. Todd could hear it in his choking, trembling voice. "You have no idea what this means to us, you sweet angel!"

Todd could tell from his voice Addison was older, which piqued Todd's curiosity about him and Harris, if they were married or just longtime partners. "That's a story for another time, my friend," Addison said, regaining his composure. "Besides, it'll give us something to talk about when we thank you in person."

When he mailed out the ring, Todd had automatically put his return address on the upper left-hand corner of the small package—a force of habit, really, and nothing more. He honestly didn't expect to ever hear from them ever again. Three months later, unbeknownst to Todd, it would lead Harris and Addison back to the Keys to meet the man who had done them such a huge favor.

When they showed up at Todd's door—two sixty-something gents who were both balding, wore glasses, and had walked up to him hand-in-hand—they'd said words couldn't describe how much they were indebted to him. Addison, the shorter of the two, as promised, explained how the ring had more significance than Todd knew. His brother, David, was the only member of the Hartley family that hadn't disowned him when he had come out to them about his sexuality. In fact, he supported both Harris and him in their life together from the beginning. Two weeks after David had bought and inscribed the rings as a gift to his brother and partner—his expression to mark the time they stopped hiding their secret love—he was killed in a tragic car accident. The ring was one of the few things Addison had left to remember him by. They both knew no other ring, even a wedding band, would have meant as much to them if it had been lost for good. They were promise rings to each other to always stay true to who they are, bravery symbolized.

As a sign of their gratitude to Todd, they bought his second priciest painting. They said it was the least they could do.

*

The swelling excitement behind discovering something that belonged to someone else and then successfully returning it to them, with the appreciation in their breaking voices and the gratefulness in their eyes, the entire experience bookended with big emotion, thrilled Todd. It also brought him to another realization that this whole thing may have been an isolated incident, but it was *real*. So, what was to stop him from doing it again?

Those moments did come more often as time went on and fueled the fire of his new habit of scouring the beaches. He knew there was a psychological conduit to his generosity and searches, as well as the high he would get when he brought lost happiness back to these people. The truth of it was, he wanted a stranger to approach *him* out of nowhere and bring back his little boy, his sweet little Kyle.

But *was* it stupid for him to think that way? Was it naïve and silly and childish and unhealthy? Was he a hopeful romantic that believed in those kinds of things? He didn't think he was. He thought he was just another parent wishing his son to come back to him, another human being who felt the stabbing heartache of someone no longer in his life. But was it so wrong to be one of those few good people left in the world with a pointless hope? What was so wrong with that, with having that kind of a reputation?

*

Weeks and months went by in a flash, causing Todd to think, not for the first time since landing in Key West, of a common turn of phrase—*Time flies when you're having fun.*

And he had to ask himself, was he? Was he actually enjoying his life to the point of happiness again, or at least, another form of it? The warm sunshine and sea salt-laden air had bleach-cleaned his lungs and skin. The exercise he had unknowingly engaged in with his walks around town and the bike rides to the beach had completely erased the office gut cultivated over years of stagnant sitting. He had lost thirty pounds since moving to Key West and he felt amazing. More often than he would have liked to admit, he had to stop in front of the mirror to admire his slimming shape, the returning definition of his jaw line and the whiteness of his eyes, now clear of those irritating red squigglies after a long week squinting at numbers on a spreadsheet. Yes, his hair had inevitably gone by the wayside, leaving him a thinning tuft on his crown. But, if he slipped on a ball cap, he was surprised how many female eyes he'd catch with a smile.

Yet Todd was enjoying life too much to consider another relationship.

Around the same time he'd noticed his improving physical changes, he was a few months deep into his routine of hitting Sloppy Joe's for a couple of beers on tap and strolling back home,

Hemingway-style. One night, while enjoying a basket of onion rings and a cold beer and talking to two lovely brunette women from Chicago who had come to his table to strike up a conversation, he had a mini epiphany. During their beer-soaked chatter, he realized, yes, he was happy once again, whatever happiness truly is.

He was fine leaving the two attractive Chicagoans at the table after some engaging conversation about the 'real world' Todd had cut himself from; the world he had left behind back on the mainland. He found all their talk funny and endlessly trivial. Nonetheless, he paid for their drinks, bid them adieu, and left them curious of his special little life as a single island painter and habitant of this strangely wonderful, tropical place.

What was that song that Jimmy Buffet sang? *"Changes in Latitudes, Changes in Attitudes"*?

When he looked back into the bar to offer a final smile to the two women, he found they were still watching him walk out of Sloppy Joe's. On the stage, the longhaired amateur singer began playing one of Mr. Buffet's songs. This, naturally, was greeted with a roar of approval from the drunken crowd.

*

Tonight, however, Todd Freeman lay in bed with the nightlife of Key West just getting started at the early hour of ten o'clock. It was warm tonight, and at the open window by his bed, a soft breeze played with the linen curtains.

Instead of a beer or two at Sloppy Joe's, he nestled closer to the pillow, his eyes on the two framed pictures of Kyle. The frames sat on the edge of his dresser, next to his bed, so that Kyle was the first person he saw when he woke up and the last person he looked upon when he went to sleep.

Todd swore never to be caught off guard by a surprise visit from his son if he unexpectedly stumbled across a picture of him.

Something Found: A Coin

Photos tended to do that—catch you off guard, that is. Hiding in drawers or slipping into mish-mashed storage areas like shoeboxes and tax return folders were common in any house. Those were always the worst, too. The surprise of it. The *unexpectedness* of it. Especially if they hadn't seen them in a few days, or even weeks. Keeping friends with ghosts might be hard and even drawn out to some, but they never jumped out at him. Todd made sure of that.

One picture on the dresser featured Kyle in his little league uniform, a bat resting on his shoulder. In the other, he wore a uniform made of military camouflage and a rifle over his opposite shoulder. It was like a couple of bizarre mirror images of past and future, facing off.

Since he had moved to Key West, most of his nights were dreamless, as this one would be. He didn't know why this was. He didn't really care to know. Nor had he thought any more about the coin he'd found earlier and had emailed Alex about. If it *was* real he would see how much he could get out of it, maybe donate it to a museum or something.

Soon, he began to snore. He'd need his rest for the challenges ahead. Todd hadn't any idea what that little coin presently sitting on his desk in the moonlight had gotten him into. Or the kind of irreversible damage that e-mail had set in motion. Or what was in store for him in the coming days. What kind of secret worlds and people he was about to meet, and encounter, and experience.

All of it was more than any metal detector could *ever* find.

CHAPTER 6

THE WARNING

IT HAD BEEN years since Todd Freeman had gotten up at six a.m. beyond an enthusiastic rooster wakeup call from the street. Todd was a night owl by nature, always had been, struggling with the early morning wake up time for his corporate career. In his opinion, some of his best artwork was done by the playful glow of the city lights and his monitor, a drink and some tunes to get the creative juices flowing. In Dayton, he'd worked under the humming florescent lighting of his dusty garage, after Emma had gone to sleep. In college, it had been under the soft blush of a weak bulb on his hand-me-down desk in his dorm, trying not to wake up his drunk and passed out roommate with pencil scratches, and the Stones and Zep rocking softly from the radio.

So, it wasn't a surprise, then, that when the phone rang with hardly any morning light in the sky, Todd woke up pissed as hell, certain it was a prank call or a wrong number.

The first ring woke him up, catching him in mid-snore and causing a comical coughing-gagging sound that probably would have been hilarious to anyone watching.

It was that second ring that pissed him off.

He picked up the receiver and cleared his throat. "Hello?"

He thought he sounded like he was talking through a mouth

full of peanut butter. That funny consideration, though, was driven from his mind by the seriousness of the unfamiliar voice on the other end.

"Where did you find it?" the voice demanded.

"What," he asked. "Who's—"

"It's Alex, man. From Miami." He slowed his words, but the serious tone never faltered. "Now, where…did you…find…it?"

Todd rubbed at his eyes, trying to wake up. With Alex awaiting an answer, Todd struggled with what he was talking about and, for that matter, who Alex even was.

Then, of course, he remembered: the tiny coin with the funny lines and the odd and ancient profile.

"Oh! Uh, okay…um…the beach, Alex, just like I always do."

"Which beach?" The tone in Alex's voice woke him up a little more.

"Uh, Higgs Beach. Yeah, Higgs. Why? What's going on? Wait…how'd you get my number?"

"You have to get out of there, your place. *Right now.* Have you been out yet? Is there a red triangle on your door? Or your car?"

"W-what? I don't, I don't know. You just woke me up, man. What are—"

"You have to come to Miami. Bring the coin."

"What? Miami? Dude, I'm not coming to Miami. Why would I? Why would I do that?"

In his answer, the solemn, grave inflection in his voice held steady, the dread coming through the receiver loud and clear. "Because, Todd, you won't have hands by noon if you don't."

"Wha—"

"By two, your feet will be fish food. When the sun goes down tonight, *if* you're still alive and you haven't completely bled out, you won't have a head to sit on your shoulders. No more sunsets, Todd. No more painting. No more art. No more anything. Listen to what I'm saying, okay? Get your ass out of there *now* or it might be too late."

"For what?" Todd sat up in bed, resting on one arm, the other cradling the phone to his ear. The white sheets fell to expose his hairy chest. His skin broke out in goosebumps, whether from the cool morning air or the sinister words coming from the phone, Todd wasn't sure.

"They might be on their way already."

"Alex—"

"*Shut up*, man! This phone call is over in twenty seconds. This line probably isn't safe so I'm not saying any more. It's open and they might be listening. Get in your car and drive. I'm gonna send you something. It's directions to someone. He's a good friend and he can explain this much better than I could. See him before you come to me. You should be safe with him. But get *out* of there. And if anyone, and I mean *anyone*, follows you too closely, you call me and I'll take care of it. That's all I can say."

Alex killed the connection and Todd pulled the phone away from his ear, staring dumbfounded at it. The call had lasted a whole fifty-eight seconds.

After tossing the phone back onto his dresser, he sat up in bed a moment longer, reflecting on the jarring call. Scratching his head and rubbing the sleep from his eyes, he felt almost delusional, even dazed, like a man jerked from a very realistic and vividly horrific dream. What kind of way was that to wake up?

Out the side window overlooking the street, the early morning sky was barely blue, but clear, the sun slow to make its first appearance. It seemed like it would be just another lovely day that would, come noon, be considered postcard-worthy. He thought he even heard the soft cooing of the family of doves that had nested in his gutters just above that window.

After struggling out of bed almost as slowly as the sun rose in the sky, he walked to the window to peek out.

Something Found: A Coin

Nothing happened. The car is fine. The street is fine. No one is out there. Nothing is out there.

Sure enough, his Buick, parked on the side of the studio, was in its usual condition. It wasn't trashed or vandalized in any way, nor was there any indication anyone was about to do any such thing. And there most certainly weren't any red triangles on it, at least that he could tell from his vantage point. What did Alex even mean by *that* question, anyway?

Dressed only in gym shorts, Todd headed downstairs to the lower studio level, where he heard the whine of his fax machine spitting out paper.

Once he reached the bottom of the stairs, the sound of the fax abruptly stopped and then started back up again, as if noticing the king had unexpectedly risen from his slumber and paused in respect for his arrival. In its tray were five sheets of paper, three of them from advertisers.

The other two were from Alex.

Todd pondered for a moment why he had sent the information to the fax if 'they might be listening'. Surely if the mysterious forces that were tracking their phone conversations had the ability and technology to bug a phone (a phone he had been near all night, so Todd was more than a little confused), they could easily see what was being faxed to him as well, right? Then he remembered that the fax line was under the studio name and that it was the only one they wouldn't be able to trace through his exact name, even though he was the sole proprietor, but only through the pseudonym Art Studio. He had separated his working life from his living one long ago, even if what he did now was thoroughly relaxing and enjoyable. Force of habit, he supposed, but even so, how was Alex able to track down and figure out that information?

One page that Alex had sent him was a printout of a Google

map screen like it was 2004, with dark sharpie arrows pointing to a spot near the water's edge roughly two-thirds the way up the chain of Keys toward the mainland. The other page was Alex's shaky script with the name Hamok Bagbarsarian—at least, he *thought* that was what it said—scrawled in blue ink. Next to it was a short description (older and stout) and the best number to get a hold of Alex in case something came up. It also gave an exact address, and explained that Hamok would be the best person to see before reaching his shop in Miami.

THEN YOU WILL UNDERSTAND, the scrawl read.

Underlined and just below all of this, in huge, gaudy letters, were the words, YOU ARE IN SERIOUS DANGER. GET OUT NOW!!

And that was it. That was all he sent.

The studio-gallery was quiet now. Outside, past the displayed canvas on its easel and through the large open picture window, Todd saw the street was empty and as silent as his studio, caught in that short void of time when the whole island closed down for four hours for the next shift of barkeeps, cooks, and inebriated party people to stroll in.

He glanced back at the map to the destination Alex had so vigorously circled: the tiny city of Isla De Oro. At this point, he was still besieged with waking up and getting his mind wrapped around this apparent stage-five tornado he'd been thrown into. Figuring the driving distance was a bit of a challenge, as he hadn't been to Miami since settling in Key West. Coming up with an ETA to a town he had never even heard of before was another.

Alex's voice haunted him nonetheless, and he knew why—it was real. Todd's instincts were pretty sharp now when it came to those kinds of things.

Peering back outside, beyond his big canvas displayed by the window, he saw nothing out of the ordinary. The same cars were parked in their regular places, the big house across the street had the second-story window fan softly rotating in the humid morning air, and the hens and chicks were already out, clucking and pecking at whatever scraps they could find. A gull flew by in the blank sky. A horn honked somewhere several blocks away. A dog barked even further away than that.

Nothing.

What did you think you were going to see, Toddy? An army of men in black suits and sunglasses ready to pillage your little studio? A parade of Hell's Angels with clubs and pipes in their hands, ready to do a number on you?

Just as it was inside, the street was quiet, calm, serene. The pale dawn didn't offer much in the way of details, but faint sunlight kissed the street and the swaying palm trees, whose rustling fronds mingled almost musically together, like a morning symphony warming up. Dew shone everywhere. The thought of there being any possibility of real, violent danger lurking around the corner seemed utterly ridiculous.

Todd left the window.

Back in his apartment upstairs, he went directly to his desk and examined the coin again, this time with scrutiny and cynicism.

How is this stupid little thing worth a trip to Miami? It's three hours away…five with traffic. Plus he wants me to see his friend…what was it?…Hackysack Barbarian?…beforehand.

YOU ARE IN DANGER. That was what the fax in his hand read.

Goddamnit Alex, what have you gotten me into? I only asked a stupid question.

He glanced at the clock. Twenty minutes had already gone by since his call. If he wanted to beat traffic, he needed to get rolling.

Todd fetched a change of clothes—brown cargo shorts, a white tank top, an unbuttoned white dress shirt with the sleeves rolled up, Ray-Bans, and his covered sandals. Then, after collecting his keys, wallet, cell phone, and of course the funny penny, he fetched some paper to leave a note for Mark.

Mark was Todd's young part-time helper, shopkeeper, social media manager, charity administrator to the Veteran aid organizations the studio and Todd personally donated to, and overall schmoozer of visiting art enthusiasts. Some of whom were scheduled to come into the studio for a few hours this very morning. He hoped he didn't hate him for bailing on such short notice.

Even as he was writing the note, leaving out his reasoning for his unexpected absence, Todd took pause, took a breath, and considered if he was actually going to go through with this.

Todd Freeman thought, *What the hell am I doing?*

CHAPTER 7

ISLA DE ORO

ON THE SHORT drive through the quiet streets of Key West, on his way toward the long stretch of US 1, Todd Freeman had to admit to himself that he felt more than a little jumpy. His emotions had evolved from passive and questioning to downright jittery when he first got behind the wheel of his car and now, finally, to outright anxiety. Locking the door to his apartment in the early light of the morning, the air already muggy as gulls called above him, made his fear authentic, real. Creeping down the outside stairs to his car, the sound of a ticking clock in his head, made it real. Getting behind the wheel (not to mention nearly jumping out of his skin to Christopher Cross's *Ride Like The Wind* blasting out of the radio when he turned the car over) and looking around the neighborhood for anything suspicious made it real. But it was driving out of town for the first time with the clear intention of making it all the way to the mainland, that made it extremely real. Bona fide, even.

In doing this, he felt like a man about to board an elevator known to have creaking gears and rusting cogs; an airplane passenger boarding the jet after a long absence of flight. Sure, there was always the risk: the elevator's cables could snap and plummet to the ground floor, or the airplane could be hijacked, or, worse, crash into a mountain, but those were the chances you took. Todd wasn't about to live in constant fear. No, he didn't know what to expect around the bend, but he tried to keep his optimism as close to his heart as the budding worries.

By the time he left the studio, moments after leaving the note for Mark taped to the computer monitor for him to see first thing, the sun had broken the horizon. Todd couldn't remember the last time he'd actually seen a sunrise.

In Todd's mind, the city of Miami was the busiest, most crowded tollbooth in the world, with three million-plus people dancing their way through its blockade of gridlocked traffic and sweaty bodies like the longest, most condensed conga line on earth. He dreaded fighting through the sticky bowels of the city. The three-hour trek up there was bad enough, but the pit stop at a complete stranger's house was salt on the wound. Dammit, was he *really* doing this?

He watched his studio and home fade away in the Buick's rearview mirror.

Yes, he was really doing this.

*

Maneuvering his big Roadmaster just a few blocks, Todd discovered the rest of the surrounding streets were virtually deserted, as well. Only a few other cars haunted the byways with him at this hour and for that he was indebted. The lack of traffic helped the situation, calming his nerves and fending off his increasing paranoia. Yet, at the same time, with every moving car he *did* pass, the heat of unshakable apprehension rose a few more degrees, setting his anxiety simmering.

Damn. Alex really did a number on me, didn't he? I mean, how crazy is this? It's just a coin! How is it worth all this trouble? Are we talking millions here? Priceless?

The street coiled east around the city's initial scattering of name brand hotels, diners, and a few locally owned bike and boat rental shops. At the crossing of Roosevelt and the beginning of the Overseas Highway—the only way in or out of Key West via a paved road—Todd swung northeast, hanging a left on to the start of U.S. 1, also known as A1A, through the tiny neighboring island of Cow Key, and past the Key West Navel Air Station, embarking on his journey toward Isla De Oro and eventually (he shuddered) Miami.

A little past the naval air station, well outside of the city and into the great wild beyond, the buildings quickly grew dilapidated and ramshackle compared to the main island's pristine and colorful resort-style architecture. For all its broken and beaten worth, Todd felt there was a certain charm to those shanties that someone like him could appreciate for the time-gone-by characteristic they humbly displayed. Old school Florida, in all its moss-ridden and hurricane-damaged glory. The *trueness* of them. The *realness* of them, as Todd would have put it.

As he ventured further beyond the outskirts of the city toward the string of other, smaller keys, the trees and thick vegetation would thin and break periodically, disclosing the shoreline only a few feet from the road. He had forgotten about that. He had forgot how wide the sky was on this drive too, how the horizon stretched out to infinity with a razor cut dividing sea and sky, how the clouds built in the southeast toward the West Indies and the Caribbean like mountains of thick whip cream. The swelling cloudscape may have looked menacing enough, but they were lazy and would most likely get caught in the northerly blow of the Gulf, temporarily blocking the blinding glare of the rising sun and allowing Todd's strained eyes a much needed break as he drove toward its shining arrival.

By the time he reached Cudjoe Key, the sun was out with a fiery orange anger, the slow, sleepy rise to the new day burning away faster than the morning mist around Upper Sugarloaf

Sound and Pirates Cove. With radiant sun illuminating A1A, and nothing obviously threatening nearby, Todd's unease gradually subsided. A few more cars passed him on the road, nobody taking more than a casual glance in his direction. Sometimes not at all.

Pushing a little harder on the gas, nonetheless, he found his car ran just as smoothly as it ever had on the interstate. The Buick had had some general repairs done to it since he had settled in the Keys—a set of new tires and an air filter, just to name a few—so with those repairs Todd's confidence in the car was solid, even with its age. At least that was *something* he felt secure in. The size of his land monster of a vehicle was enough for him to know that if anyone tried anything threatening on this trip, he would more than likely have the upper hand by sheer girth alone.

What did give him pause soon after Cudjoe Key was the newer Ford Crown Victoria behind him that could have been mistaken for an unmarked patrol car. Even so, he still tensed up, preparing for an ambush.

An ambush? Jesus, am I already thinking like that? Get a grip, man. You got out of your place like he asked; how would they know what your car looks like too? Or where you're at exactly?

Todd's eyes switched from the rearview mirror to the road ahead of him. He had set his speed at a steady, law-abiding sixty-three miles an hour. Though, it wasn't but a few miles later that the driver of the Ford revealed herself when she sped into the passing lane. It was an old woman with enormous Martini glasses for bifocals and white, cottony hair. By the way she gripped the steering wheel, she appeared to be holding on for dear life.

After checking his shirt pocket again for the hundredth time, fingering the weight and shape of the coin through the cloth, and noticing nothing suspicious around him, Todd's senses began to teeter between the odd combination of high alertness and foolishness. He started to feel silly, and not just because of the old lady speeding past him. It was the whole shebang. He was feeling like the center of a prank, or maybe Alex was in on some reality show and had chosen him to be a kind of lucky patsy. Unlikely, but who knew? After almost ninety minutes in the car with the most threatening aspect of his jaunt being some strong wind gusts over a couple of bridges to rock his station wagon, Todd's nerves hadn't only settled, but his suspicions had all but fallen away. Honestly, had Alex told him to drive straight to Miami and not to Isla De Oro first—still two hours away from his home, but close enough to get back before noon—he would have chalked it up to an extremely late April Fool's joke and turned around at the next off-shooting island side street.

Yet, he drove on.

Next to the coin was his cell phone, a flip he rarely used nowadays. In Dayton, in his old life, his secured smart phone had been an asset, but also a personal ball and chain. The only reason he had one now was for the studio and, of course, the base reason we all excuse ourselves for having constant wireless connectivity: in case of emergency. So, when he purchased one, he made sure the primary function was making calls and not much else. No e-mail, Internet access, or apps. Nothing. Free Man, thy name is Freeman.

After a quick glance at his phone to see if Alex had tried to contact him—he hadn't—he slipped it back in his pocket.

It was just before Big Pine Key that he wished for some kind of weapon. Even though Alex had reassured him to call if he needed help, he didn't like the idea of harking for aid like a dummy if he found himself in a bind. Self-sufficiency was something Todd took pride in. But he didn't have any defenses to bring, other than maybe steak knives from his kitchen, and that just seemed entirely too messy and primitive.

As he navigated the length of Seven Mile Bridge alone, and pushed through the city of Marathon with one eye on the road and one on his rearview mirror, the sun continued to push up into the sky. Spotting more people in Marathon as the morning pressed on, the anxiety of everything came right back to him, rejuvenated and strong as ever in the presence of people. It felt like everyone he saw was looking at him, and for the umpteenth time, he wondered just what the hell he'd gotten himself into.

*

According to the directions on the map Alex had faxed him, Hamok's house in Isle De Oro was less than a mile away, stationed on that tiny two-mile blip of an island between the cities of Marathon and Islamorada. The drive had taken longer than he'd expected. But this was also his first trip up the chain of islands, so of course it was going to take longer than expected.

A greater, budding anxiety grew in Todd now, and he felt antsy to get to Alex in Miami; for answers, yes, but mainly because he was already halfway there. So why this stopover? Was the detour to his friend's place just a strategic distraction, of sorts? As he closed in on his halfway-point destination, the questions began to surface faster and harder.

Between his panic, anxiety, and the engine running on all cylinders in his head, he couldn't deny there was also a growing, somewhat ravenous curiosity over the coin. Friction and novelty pumped from that engine as different wild theories swam laps in Todd's head on his drive here, from a long, lost coin from a Roman ship connected to a Drug Lord stationed in the Keys to a fabled, forgotten doubloon like Davis had suggested just last night. There was the random and irrational thought that this was somehow connected back to Jeremy Patrick, exacting revenge from beyond his prison walls for finding his crowbar, but Todd couldn't formulate a logical connection to the two. In any case, the word *priceless* danced seductively in his mind. If his life was in danger just for having it in his possession, it had to be worth *something*. But enough to torture and kill him over, too? Jesus Christ!

Even though Alex said Hamok was the man to see, he still

felt uncomfortable going to the house of a complete stranger. He reminded himself, as a bit of comfort as he pulled into the Isla De Oro city limits, that Alex had said he would inform Hamok of his visit beforehand. Still, if he was suddenly dealing with murderers and decapitators, meeting new folks wasn't at the top of his bucket list at the moment.

A big, cement-mixer truck had slowed him down considerably over the past four miles. Before he knew it, there was a line of cars behind him that seemed to stretch forever, and he questioned every one of the drivers, debating which one was brandishing a sword in the passenger seat long enough to take his head off.

There was a patch of residential streets off US 1 that he presumed led straight to the shoreline. Soon after crossing into Isla De Oro, Todd found the street name he had been looking for, the one circled on the map printout. He eased the Buick down the nearly silent street off the main road and took a deep breath.

With this turn, he was suddenly enveloped in a canopy of lush trees and bushes, as if the Amazonian jungle had just swallowed him whole. Sunrays couldn't make it through the green ceiling of coconut palm fronds and wide thatch leaves, and the temperature noticeably cooled here.

Down the short street were only a few houses, all of them sitting on molded, aged stilts and invaded by thriving and fertile vegetation, before the tranquil dead end of the water's edge. Overgrown bougainvillea and sea grape carpeted the ground, even crept up the stilts of the homes like some hustler's wandering fingers sneaking up a skirt. Here and there, he spotted clusters of pineapple plants and blooming hibiscus dotting the scenery with gracious amounts of contrasting color, reminding him of a Jackson Pollock painting by way of the Caribbean. It was lovely and abundant and striking, but most of all it was distracting to what he should have been focusing on—who might be behind him. Who might be following him…

He peered in the rearview mirror, thankful to see the long line of cars behind the cement mixer continue without turning. He slowed to a stop on the side of the vacant island road, watching the cars roll by behind him. With the last car on the A1A passing, the silence of the street wasn't just deep now, but eerily encompassing, even more so than Key West had been a little over two hours before in the pale sunrise.

After double-checking the address on the fax printout, and after closer inspection of the map, Todd found it was the last house before the street either curved to the right or ran into a small dock. The curve of the street was there, as was the dock which, with the early morning light glistening on the water, positively begged for fishermen.

As if on cue, a fish broke the calm surface, gone as quickly as it had come and the only sign of life anywhere near him.

The whole area made him uneasy despite its astounding beauty. Was there something else, something unsettling about the street and the houses he wasn't picking up on yet? As he approached the home, Todd believed there was—he just couldn't put his finger on it.

Hamok's house lacked a numerical address. Or, if it did have one, the overgrowth hid it. The roof had leaf piles of various shapes and sizes, layers of dead brown muck like some moldy lasagna. Fuzzy green moss grew at the top and down the side. If the dead leaves on the roof were the lasagna, then this was its cheesy runoff, staining the siding of the house the color of cartoon toxic waste. The house itself was supported by stilts that looked worn and rickety and ready to collapse, just like the rest of the lineup on this grove-like street. Which, after a quick count, was only four other homes spread widely apart. A single Royal Palm stood in front of Hamok's stilted shack, and Todd thought he even spotted decorative bricks surrounding it, as if at one time the owner had *tried* to improve the exterior, but had given up on that dream long ago. All in all, Todd was amazed the house was even standing at all—the Ritz-Carlton, it was not.

One, maybe two more hard blows from the Sea Gods and this baby's going down hard, he thought, parking the car. He pulled the Buick to the side of the street, half on the grass and half on the road, not wanting to disrespect the man by just pulling into his driveway. People were touchy about those sorts of things.

After a moment of closer observation, he figured out what that strange feeling was, the one he couldn't put a finger on a moment ago: Hamok's home was a Floridian haunted house. It was the Overlook Hotel, Hill House, and the Winchester Mansion through the eyes of Carl Hiaasen or Elmore Leonard, compacted, stilted, and printed on a beach setting postcard.

Taking another deep breath and tossing his sunglasses onto the passenger seat, he unfastened his seatbelt and got out of the car, noting again the incredible silence of the street. The hollow, faraway sound of passing cars at the other end where it met up with the U.S. 1 was the only real noise of any kind, and it sounded far away. No birds. No bugs. Nothing. Not even the leaves rustled against each other. It was like being transported to some empty, vacuuming void.

Walking up the driveway, leaves crunching underfoot—which, in the eerie stillness, sounded no louder than pirate-ship canon blasts with each footfall—he questioned if a pair of nasty pit bulls would suddenly stampede around the cluster of rusted oil barrels under the house, teeth barred and jowls flapping. Todd saw no paw marks in the sandy dirt, so that brought some relief. The driveway that led to the stilted structure was littered with patches of sea grass, dustings of white sand, and pieces of leaves like flyers and cigarette butts after a concert. Even a couple of oil leaks had stained the cement for good measure.

He was halfway up the dirt drive when he heard the door of the house start to rattle open. Todd stopped. A disturbing image passed though his head: a man with a loaded shotgun busting out the front door, screaming profanities and aiming the weapon squarely at him.

Instead, when it did open, a squat little old man in a wifebeater shirt, with thinning salt and pepper hair and scrawny legs, came out, breathing heavily and shutting the door behind him with a slam. Todd assumed he was either trying to keep an animal of some kind inside, or the door didn't close properly from lack of repair. The man walked out onto his lifted porch with his head down, as if he were looking at his feet.

"Hello?" Todd called, not seeing a weapon in his hands from this vantage point, but not taking any chance of surprising the guy, either. He could hear the wood of the lifted porch creaking under the man's weight.

When the old man reached the end of the balcony, slowly maneuvering around the filthy covered grill and carefully placing his hands on its weathered ledge, he finally looked down to meet Todd's eyes.

The first thing that struck Todd was how wide the man's face was. His eyes were large too, and deeply hazel, the whites just visible from where Todd was standing. At the top of the warped steps leading down to the driveway, he seemed to study Todd with a curt, dubious expression.

"Were you followed?" There was an accent there, but Todd couldn't place it. Greek, maybe?

Todd blinked. He looked back at his car, then down the quiet, empty street, and then back up at the older man. "I don't think so," he answered. He couldn't help it: his voice slipped into a mildly joking tone at the grave way the old man was acting in such a serene and peaceful environment. But the older gent caught it immediately, pausing halfway down the steps with a mixture of stern grandfatherly sharpness and suspicion.

"It's a yes or no question."

"Well then, my answer is no."

The old man appeared dubious, pausing at the halfway point on the steps before sighing and continuing his elderly, one-step-at-a-time struggle down to ground level. "So, you're Todd Freeman?"

"Yes."

"I'm Hamok," he said, and reached the bottom of the steps, gingerly choosing his footing right to the very end. "Like the netted thing you sleep in."

Todd nodded. "Obliged."

When Hamok hit ground level he paused and hitched up another great sigh, probably glad to have safely touched down.

"Bring your car in here," he said, gesturing length-wise with a boney hand to the driveway. "We have to cover it to be sure."

Todd tilted his head thoughtfully at this before agreeing and walking back to his car, wondering what Hamok had in mind. Hamok, meanwhile, slowly meandered under the house to one of the main support stilts elevating his home. There was a pile of something Todd couldn't decipher near the post, on a stack of boxes and crates near the cluster of oil barrels. As he looked back at him from his car, Todd saw they were large tarp coverings that matched the tanned hue of Hamok's skin.

Todd got in his car, automatically checking his pocket for the coin once more, and swung his Buick into the drive where Hamok waited. He noticed Hamok had a swollen belly and hairy arms. Under all that hair, there looked to be a scribble of a tattoo—of what, he had no idea. Hamok guided Todd into the open spot next to his own battered vehicle, before signaling him to stop.

Unfolding the tarp and walking past Todd's open window, Hamok said nonchalantly, "They come in unmarked cars, sometimes like police."

"Who does?" Todd stood and slipped his keys back into his pocket. He thought about the old woman with cotton soft hair and Martini-sized glasses who'd driven around him earlier in what he thought was an unmarked patrol car.

"Not all of them, but most of them do. They think they're hiding in plain sight, but if you know what to look for, it's obvious."

"I'm not following you."

"Here. Help me with this." Hamok handed Todd one corner of the tarp as he began pulling it over his Buick, ignoring Todd's inquiry. Todd noticed Hamok continually glancing up the street toward the main highway as he covered the front section of his car. There weren't any vehicles passing by and the air remained as silent as a cemetery on Christmas morning. Todd gathered it was normally like this, with the water's edge not three hundred feet from the home, a tranquil refuge if he had ever seen one. But he also figured Hamok's nerves must have been working overtime, given his suspiciousness. If he had woken up to Alex calling him with the same deadly warnings and threats, maybe his old blood was just as riled up. Then again, maybe that was just his nature.

Once the tarp covered most of the Buick, Hamok brought over some potted plants that looked near death. The leaves were brown and withered, the dirt appearing old and starved for nutrients. Hamok set the plants on the hood and the roof.

"What's this for?"

"Disguise," Hamok said, and Todd heard the faint accent for a second time. Hamok unfolded the other tarp—his short stubby fingers struggling with it—and then he and Todd covered the big bubble butt back of the wagon. Hamok then did something that caused Todd's eyebrows to rise to half-mast: he took two large scoopfuls of the driveway's loose, sandy dirt and began spreading it over the car evenly.

Hamok cracked a weak smile at Todd when he caught his confused expression. In that smile, Todd could see that, at one time, long ago, Hamok had been a good-looking young man. "It adds to the age. Grab some leaves and palms and throw them up there." He was wagging a finger to the car's hood.

"Okay…" Todd did as he was told, gathering some dried-out sea grape and a couple of tennis racket-sized palm fronds from the front yard. Hamok backed away after Todd had scattered the leaves as he was instructed, along with some more dirt over the now-filthy tarp covering the Buick.

"There," Hamok said, crossing his arms and sounding satisfied. "Looks like it's been here awhile. It'll buy us some time, anyway, if they do show up." Hamok then glanced back down his driveway. "Oh! Almost forgot."

He trotted down the drive and began shuffling his small feet over the tracks the Buick had made. Hamok looked funny doing this little dance in the dirt with his round belly and short legs. Todd wanted to laugh, but only smiled at the sight as he adjusted the other tarp for effect, trying to look busy.

After he was finished, Hamok looked over the covered car once more and smiled, returning to the same expression of smug satisfaction.

Todd approached him and surveyed the quick job they had done together as strangers. Hamok then turned and put out his hand. "Pleased to meet you, good sir."

"Likewise." They shook, both men equally firm in their grip, with Todd producing his customary crooked smile.

"Come, please. We must get out of the open, where there are ears for listening and eyes for watching."

*

Todd followed Hamok, who had already started up the first few steps of his rundown house. Todd noticed that when Hamok had descended the stairs he leaned heavily on his right leg, but when he ascended the steps he only used his left leg to do the job, carefully placing his foot on the step and pushing up, doing the same action with the same foot, all fourteen steps.

"Don't worry, it will be fine," Hamok said, waving a hand at the car and looking down at Todd with a smile from the halfway point of the climb. He nodded his head to join him up top. "You can come up here. I won't bite."

Todd started to climb the porch steps to follow him, wondering for the millionth time what he was getting himself into with this polite, albeit peculiar, stranger. Since he was downwind from Hamok, he caught a soft whiff of something he couldn't identify.

"When Alex called me this morning, I thought he was pulling my leg, as the American saying goes," Hamok said, reaching the top of the stairs and opening the front door. As he did, Todd caught a final glimpse of his car from the top of the stairs. It was true: the car looked like it had been sitting in that spot for years; the leaves and dirt were a nice touch.

"Oh yeah?"

"Yes. I was already awake, watching my shows. *M*A*S*H* is always on early, so I was watching that, but I hadn't made my coffee yet. I still haven't made any, in fact. His call woke me up more than ten cups and a cold shower could have. But I would be a rude host to not offer you a cup. Would you like some?"

"Coffee? No thanks," Todd said. "His call did the same for me, believe me. I think my car could've run on my nerves all the way up here."

"Oh?" Hamok passed the threshold of his front door with an expression of the most interest he had shown in Todd yet, eyes lit and eyebrows high. Curious. Intrigued.

Todd followed him and was greeted with the strongest scent of what he hadn't been able to identify, until that moment. It was ham, honey baked. A man named *Ham*ok who smells of pork? What are the odds? "Then you understand the gravity of the situation, no? I assume you brought it with you. The coin?"

"Yes…I was…shaken…but I'm going to be honest with you. I'm completely foggy over what this is all about. What's the story behind it? What's it worth?"

Hamok actually stopped and made sure they were looking at each other in the eyes when he spoke. "More than you know, young man. More than you could know." Then, Hamok waddled deeper into the house before throwing a wave over his shoulder to follow him further.

Inside the fragrant house, the floors creaked, naturally. Hardly expecting a palace within, Todd was indeed greeted with copious amounts of clutter and the leavings of an aged packrat. What little light broke through the old curtains didn't illuminate much of anything, so shadows of thirsty houseplants and worn furniture and what looked like a wooden statue of a Pacific island god were Todd's first impressions of Hamok's decorative tastes. The underlying odor of a house pet filled his nostrils and the sounds of TV commercials drifted though the musty air.

Hamok plopped down in an aged recliner in the corner. There, he faced the small tube television where he apparently was still watching his old reruns. Todd always hated morning and daytime television, but as Hamok reached for the remote on the cluttered table, a newscaster was giving a preview of the noonday news.

"…and with donations from Miami's Almost Billionaire Zachary M—"

Mercifully, Hamok turned off the television.

"Have a seat," Hamok offered the couch next to him, which was situated in front of the biggest window and the only real source of natural light in the living room. Hamok then started rummaging over the cluttered end table next to his chair, lifting messy stacks of papers and small prescription vials—the station of every elderly man the world over. He found what he was looking for, his trifocals, and slipped them on halfway up the bridge of his nose, their dulled gold chain swinging just below his face.

"Now, I don't have my hopes up. This is a million to one shot and the likelihood you found it so easily is cause for a chuckle. On the other hand, Alex has never steered me wrong before." Hamok watched him over the glasses, awaiting the coin.

"He sounded pretty serious this morning," said Todd, who stepped over a stack of binders, books, and loose papers on his way to the couch.

Out of the corner of his eye, Todd caught movement low to the floor. A fat tabby cat appeared from one of the other back rooms, presumably the bedroom where it was enjoying a midmorning snooze, curious about the new visitor. The cat looked around, eyed Todd, blinked, and yawned.

He accepted Hamok's offer of the couch. Hamok's demeanor reminded Todd too much—almost eerily—of his own father.

Todd reached into his shirt pocket as he settled onto the couch and causally found the coin next to his phone. Seeming equally curious, the cat approached him this time, purred deeply, and hopped onto the couch next to Todd, as if to take a gander too. Briefly examining the rusted piece of metal a final time, Todd handed it over to Hamok's eager and open palms.

The old man's eyes seemed to grow to the size of softballs. Hamok's wrinkled and now-trembling hands cupped together like a peasant humbly accepting their handout, delicately handling the disked trinket.

Hamok's own mouth opened slowly as if to speak, but nothing was said. Todd thought he heard the old man shudder instead.

"Alex..." he finally muttered, "wasn't kidding...was he?" The last part came out in an exasperated sigh of...relief? Todd wasn't sure. Hamok looked up from his hands for just the smallest of moments, as if reassuring himself this was really happening with Todd's presence still in front of him.

Todd didn't know what to say to Hamok's wide-eyed reaction. He didn't know what to think, either. So, he began casually stroking the cat's back. Hamok started digging around the end table again. This time, he produced a magnifying glass that looked about as old as Hamok himself and held it over his palm, turning the coin over to its face, with the profile of the Romanesque soldier.

"In the triangle..." Hamok said this in a whisper that Todd just barely caught.

"Triangle?" Todd asked, flatly.

Hamok hitched a breath and held it, before asking, "Todd, where did you find this?"

"On a beach. Higgs Beach, actually. Yesterday evening."

"It was just lying there in the sand?"

"Yes."

Hamok looked at him in the eye, this time more on purpose, as if sizing him up. Then it was back to staring down at the coin. "Todd, let me ask you something."

"Shoot." He had sat back against the couch, waiting for Hamok to continue, shockingly and suddenly relaxed in this environment.

"Do you have any secrets?"

Todd stuck out his bottom lip. "Who doesn't?"

One man's trash...

Todd looked at him for a moment, unsure as to what he was asking, or to what he was referring. Hamok looked back up at him, briefly, his face set with the same utmost seriousness as when they'd first met. Another size-up.

Then, examining the coin one more time, like he could barely take his eyes off it, Hamok asked, "Do you think you can keep another?"

*

"We're getting older," Hamok said. "We're up there in years, all of us. Except the secrets are dying with us, too."

Todd cocked an eyebrow but didn't respond.

"In fact, there are only a handful of us left. We're removed from the rest of the world, more than you think. Did you know people have been searching for this coin for years, decades? And you're here, sitting on my sofa, telling me you found this on a beach, a simple *beach*, in Key West? You're not one of them, are you? Or are you government? Honestly, tell me, I'm on your side."

Todd gave him a puzzled look. "What are you—"

"Nevermind. Todd, listen to me, you're still a young man; at least, compared to me. I don't see any reason not to let you in. Passing the torch, as the saying goes." Hamok looked up at him, clutching the coin and the magnifying glass and added, "You were obviously chosen for this. Maybe you're the next generation."

Todd had held the confused expression as he looked at the older man, causing Hamok to chuckle at the sight.

"My, you really are lost, aren't you? Okay."

And before Todd could answer, Hamok reached behind his back one more time. Todd thought he was going to merely scratch at his side or tuck in his shirt, so when Hamok pulled out the enormous curved blade—or it could have been a small sword, Todd wasn't sure—he automatically reacted with both hands up, jumping away to the other side of the couch, and knocking over a stack of books and binders. The fat tabby reacted by skittering off the couch and disappearing into the confines of the house in a patter of paws.

Despite the knee-jerk reaction from Todd, Hamok didn't stand or even point the huge knife at him. In fact, now Hamok was the one that wore the expression of surprised confusion at such a terrified response. Hamok froze. The blade shone against the small trickle of morning light that crept through the faded blinds.

"Whoa, I was just told to come here, man! Please don't cut off my hands! Please, I was just told—"

"It's all right, I'm not going to harm you." Hamok slowly

raised his hands, palms up, with the blade balanced on his knee. "You have my word," Hamok reassured him, and placed the long knife slowly on the table with the rest of the clutter.

Todd watched the knife anyway, as if it were going to come to life and slice him at the wrists. Or the ankles. Or the jugular. It took him a minute, but eventually Todd crawled back to left-of-center of the couch, his heart still racing.

"It's okay, it is. I'm on your side. Don't get me wrong, I understand your caution."

"Do you?" Todd snapped.

"What Alex told you was true. They will take your parts, one by one. They can be vicious and heartless, depending. I'm glad you already understand that."

"Understand? No. Cautious? Yes."

Hamok laughed, and clapped his hands in the air in a single loud snap. "You are a smart man for your age, I'll give you that one."

After a moment, Todd joined him, chuckling nervously, but unsure why. Todd's eyes darted again to the big blade on the table, all two feet of it. For all its sinister worth, the sparkling rainbow of colored jewels encrusted in the hilt was extremely attractive, especially now that he was able to truly see it on the table. The blade was about three inches longer than Todd's hand and looked about as sharp as any clean off the manufacturing floor.

"Todd, before I tell you the secret, the *greatest* secret of all, let me ask you a question: for all intents and purposes, do you believe in the fantastic? The unreal?"

Todd glanced at the floor and considered the question. "You mean ghosts? Or spirits?"

Hamok stuck out his bottom lip and shook his head, waving his hand as if to say *Posh!* "Disappearances, my friend. Missing persons never heard from again. Airplanes and ships missing from the face of the Earth without a trace. You don't think it's all chance that it happens in one spot, so often, do you?"

Todd's expression relaxed a little, as did his instincts with the knife, which was now within reach of his own hand. What was this old man blathering on about? Greatest secrets?

"Uh…are you talking about…like, sunken treasure?"

"In a sense. The Triangle, son," Hamok said. "This coin is the key to the mysteries of the Bermuda Triangle. The missing piece."

Todd blinked. "*That's* the key to the Bermuda Triangle?" Todd pointed to Hamok's hand. "A penny?"

"It's not a penny, not by any means, my friend," said Hamok. "This is the final piece of a grand map to something much bigger than you or I." Hamok paused and looked as if he was studying Todd, the tip of his tongue touching his upper lip in consideration. "Come with me."

It took Hamok a moment to get to his feet, scooting his backside to the edge of the recliner and finding his balance. Once he was on his feet, after a struggle, he moved with a little more speed, waddling from side to side as the floors beneath him groaned and squalled under the weight. As he was about to cross into a hallway that led deeper into the house, the cat rounded the corner, quickly crouched, and reacted to the body mass making its way through the house. The cat sped back to where it came as quickly as it rounded the corner, making way for its marching, giant master.

Hamok was about to cross the doorway of another room when he stopped, putting a hand on the doorframe for balance. He glanced back at Todd, who was still seated on the lumpy couch. "Before I forget, I hope you're not allergic to Bermuda."

"I've never been there."

"I meant the cat." Hamok gave him his fatherly smile again, one that was strange to see on the homely face of a stranger he'd only just met. But it was oddly comforting. Reassuring even.

"Come on. I have to show you something." With that, he gave that same wave, beckoning him deeper into his home.

Todd rose from the couch and followed Hamok to the south side of the house to a small room at the middle of the hallway... the study of a man completely obsessed.

The room was wallpapered with newspaper clippings and printed web articles from floor to ceiling. The south end was lined with tables piled with open books of a variety of sizes and ages, which Todd picked up from the ripened scent of old paper, a smell that actually overpowered the sharp stench of ham wafting through the rest of the house.

All of Hamok's stilted abode may have felt like any other that an old hermit called home, but this room was ripe with the scent of knowledge, deep analysis, history, and research—decades worth in that old paper Todd smelled. Hours upon hours had been spent in this room, poured over books and maps. This newspaper nest before him made Todd think of an obsessive professor on the brink of cracking a code, or an infatuated fan's holy shrine to their idol. In the center of the room was a massive oak desk covered by smaller nautical maps, clippings, and books. Photographs, new and ancient, dotted the walls in a random tapestry.

But the centerpiece of the room behind the desk was a huge detailed map of the Florida Keys, the Caribbean Sea with all its islands, with thin, wavy white lines in the ocean that Todd presumed were depths or topography, and large, gaudy, blue lines forming the outline of the Bermuda Triangle.

"'A single day and night of misfortune.' That's what that tale spoke of. And even though that old scribbler Plato was in another continent on the other side of the world, he knew what was going on." Hamok went to the table and started searching through the opened books and looking under the stacks of papers.

"I've heard that before. I just don't know where," Todd commented, taking in the details of the room's fanatical personality.

There was a sizeable, illustrated map of a crescent-shaped island Todd didn't recognize, a picture that looked like a drawing of a strange-looking box with deep grooved lines in it (an ancient black and white photo hung next to it, featuring four men huddled together to hold the actual odd-looking box), and a couple of pictures with what looked like varying sizes of the same giant, bejeweled knife Hamok had pulled out in the living room.

"Greek mythology has tapped into the world's imagination, Todd. But that story has a truth. A very large truth regarding the lost continent." Under one of his stacks, Hamok found a small key.

"The lost...continent?" Todd asked, looking at one of the opened books on the desk, and then into Hamok's eyes. "What do you mean?"

"The evidence is there. The only question is: do you *believe* it?" He pulled a massive book out from the very stack hiding the key.

"Hold on. What are you telling me I've found?"

"This information may be a secret we keep close to our hearts—the ones who know about it—but even we don't have all the answers, Todd. However, your coin is crucial." Hamok bent over the massive, open book he laid open on the table. "Come." And then Hamok did that same familiar wave to invite him around the desk.

Todd followed and looked at the opened pages with the older man, suddenly feeling drained of strength. Within the open tome was a highly detailed, two-page map of the Bahamas, displaying islands, geographic coordinates, small towns, and even indicating where various underwater ridges and cliffs were formed. Dotted throughout the map were red markings that Todd could only presume were the ships and planes that had disappeared in the Bermuda Triangle. Hamok's finger pointed to a circled destination on the map, where there was only the blue Caribbean Sea.

"This is where it will happen, I promise you. All my research has told me this is the place."

"Where what will happen? Why?"

"There you will find a gateway, *the* Gateway. But we must be careful, because from my understanding, from all my research, there will be a Guardian. They're gatekeepers to the grand—"

"What's a Gateway? Or a Guardian, for that matter? W-why are you telling me this? What is... what is this all about? Aw God, did I come all the way up here because of a group of conspiracy theorists? Is that what this is? I thought I was getting an estimate on this coin, or at least a logical explanation on why I'm being hunted for it." Todd's impatience had reached a boiling point at the nonsense this old man was espousing. He felt left out of a joke. Or that he was the joke. Did Hamok think he was stupid? Did he actually expect him to believe any of this? How did Alex scare him into delivering this stupid coin to an insane old man?

"Todd, you need to start accepting and understanding a new reality: you have been chosen for something very special and things are already in motion. Things are about to change drastically and you need to be ready. The sea has found you to pass the torch. I have been chasing this my entire life. My father did too, as did his father. I was taught for years, since the *cradle*, hearing these stories and legends, like a faith in of itself. The knowledge has been passed on through generations of men and women and we have been keeping the rest of the world out for many good reasons, for their own protection and quality of life. But the sea chose *you* to continue in this, son."

Todd could only stare at him. "*What?* All because I found a penny in the sand?"

Hamok looked as if he had been slapped. "This coin is no penny, by any means! And if you knew what was involved in keeping this information out of the wrong hands, *you* would have more appreciation and respect for it!"

"I'm sorry, but whose hands? Who's involved?" Todd felt the beginnings of Office Manager Todd Freeman coming out, looking for answers and logic and critical thinking.

"This government, foreign governments, well-informed pirates willing to sell the information to them...others. *That's* whose hands. If this information were given away for free, the whole world would be a very, *very* different place than the one we live in now, my friend—one that neither of us would want to live in. Believe me."

Todd rubbed the corners of his eyes before moving to his temples. "Hamok...I'm sorry, but I'm just going to say it: this is all sounding completely absurd. Is there a price tag on it, or have I just wasted my whole morning coming up here?"

Hamok slapped his hands down on the desk in a boom before looking at him square in the face with an intense air of irritation. Todd glared right back.

"Haven't you ever thought that it's mighty strange an entire *continent* hasn't been found for thousands of years? That one day it was gone, *disappeared*, and everything anyone ever knew about it was lost, yet...*yet*...every seafaring society from the corners of the earth has some kind of legend of it?"

Still, Todd stared.

"Haven't you ever thought it more than a little odd," Hamok continued, "that people have disappeared in that triangular region of the sea and have never been heard from again, with next to no evidence why? Haven't you ever thought that they might be lost for a purpose? That maybe...maybe they even *wanted* to be lost? That perhaps they're hiding from the rest of the world for a reason?"

Todd could only blink and scoff. "You're joking, right?"

Hamok held his scornful stare, nostrils flaring and his eyes ready to pop. So, Todd continued:

"And with this coin...I'm going to take a stab and say that you're purposing it's in the Bermuda Triangle?"

"I'm not *purposing* or *suggesting* anything, young man. I'm here to tell you and you came of your own will. So say it, Todd."

Todd looked at him but remained silent.

"Say it," Hamok repeated. "Say its name."

"Atlantis?"

Now, it was Hamok's turn to play the mute. A grin began curling up the corners of his mouth, revealing aged, crooked, Stonehenge teeth. Todd just wasn't sure if such a grin was out of satisfaction—or complete psychosis.

"Okay, now, how am I supposed to take you seriously? Alex sent me here with my life on the line over that thing." Todd pointed to the funny penny (he couldn't get past that title and didn't think he ever could, although *damned penny* was starting to sound more suited to his aggravation), which was still clutched in Hamok's fist. "Or that someone's on my ass to chop my head off, or something, I don't know. He just told me to get on the road. Not get a story about..." Todd dismissively threw his hands in the air. "...I don't *know* what. I mean, really? *Atlantis?*"

"This is a fact you need to accept, son," Hamok said stiffly. "For centuries, ships and fighter planes have lost contact whenever traveling through the Triangle, with strange objects of light flying in front of their fields of vision. For years there were legends that there were tidal waves, rogue waves as they're known today, that would suddenly rise up out of the ocean. This came to be thought of as an old sea tale because it sounded so ridiculous. Giant waves, forming out of thin air? Except, now the world has the technology" (Hamok's accent peeked out again in this word) "to *know* that this is not a legend, but *fact*. Why have such things been spoken of as far back as Christopher Columbus on his voyage here? *Why?*"

"I don't know, Hamok. Maybe it's because some things in the

world were never meant to be known by us." Todd said it just as a passing comment, but he knew before he even finished, it was precisely what Hamok wanted to hear.

"*Exactly!*" Hamok exclaimed, as he pointed a long, wrinkled finger at Todd. "Now you're on the right track." When he said *track* the Turkish or Mediterranean accent slipped out again.

Hamok went on. "Keeping these secrets out of the public view while staying under the radar ourselves is critical for us. That is what's truly important here—hiding the immense *power*."

"Wait a minute, what secrets? Stop talking so *cryptic* for one goddamn minute! Please!" Todd couldn't believe he was shouting at someone he'd met not twenty minutes ago, and in the guy's own house, no less. The upper management part of him was definitely coming out and he needed to temper it before he said something he regretted.

But even with Todd raising his voice, Hamok didn't seem to react or grow agitated in the slightest. In fact, from the zeal in his eyes, the excited tremor in his voice, it seemed like Hamok was reveling in this discussion. How often did the old man actually get to talk about any of this?

"Make no mistake," Hamok said, his voice graver, "*that* is the kind of passion you will need for this journey ahead of you, young man." Then, holding his stare, Hamok cracked another small, knowing smile. "I hope you're ready."

Todd took a deep breath. He could feel the blood rushing to his face and he realized this was something he hadn't felt in sometime.

"Why do you think Atlantis was lost?" Hamok asked, casually, nonchalantly. It was if he were asking where he could have misplaced his keys, or how to get to the local hardware store, or where the hot dogs were in the fridge. It broke Todd's anger and he actually had to fight off laughter at such a bluntly asinine question.

"If I knew that, Hamok, I'd be world famous." Todd glanced around the room again, this time with a more reproving eye. Then he strolled to the eastside window that looked out over the small, lush jungle just outside Hamok's house. A section of ocean peeked through the foliage, a sailboat passing by on its calm surface.

"That's not entirely true. If it were, I would be naked on the cover of *Vogue*. Believe me."

At the window, Todd let go and did laugh this time. Recovering from such a…mental image, he put his hands on his hips and stared out at the faraway sailboat. He wasn't sure where this bizarre and *completely* unexpected conversation was leading, but in spite of his simmering frustration with Hamok and all his outlandish things he had spoken of so far this morning…he actually found he was becoming more and more intrigued by his story. If there were any truth in it, he wouldn't know what to do next, where to go, or how to begin with the questions. Atlantis? Todd knew as much about Atlantis as Quantum Mechanics and fifteenth century French Literature. Besides, the whole notion being a famous, unproven fable like Bigfoot or aliens at Area 51 didn't help Hamok's argument, either. And yet, here he was, telling Todd that little coin he'd found in the sand barely half a day ago would lead him to finding the answers to this legend. It was a lure if there ever was one. And, naturally, he did yearn for more, mostly out of curiosity, or maybe for chuckles at this point. But he wasn't going forward without a healthy dose of skepticism. *Another man's treasure* may have been his mantra for the last few years, but he still knew a thing or two about being fooled. You don't earn a nickname like King Solomon of Key West without being able to read people. Hamok, though? He seemed like the genuine article. Todd couldn't recall even his own artwork giving him as much delight and conviction as "Atlantis" did Hamok.

"In all seriousness, Todd, Alex sent you here for a reason. Let me explain to you why."

Todd sighed. "Go on."

"As I was saying, I was chosen by the sea, from my lineage, and there are many of us that were put in place to help others like us. Seekers, pirates, the government, they are the ones wanting to exploit the knowledge that we have fought so hard to hide and protect."

"And you're willing to tell *me*, of all people? I literally just met you."

"I told you, Todd. The sea *chose* you with that coin. Not me. I didn't choose anyone. That coin led you to me." Hamok said this and then bent over to the side of his desk. The old man's back popped like a champagne bottle. Or maybe it was his knees.

"Actually, Alex sent me to you, but who's keeping score, right?"

From underneath the littered desk, Hamok brought out a smooth, cherry wood box and sat it on top of the stacks of papers and maps. There was a large lock on the face and Todd couldn't help but think the wood box looked like a miniaturized treasure chest. Hamok continued, "It's the same way the sea chose me, my friend."

He took the gold key he found under the books and slipped it in the lock, the very kind Todd had used on his high school locker. When Hamok pulled the lock off with a quick jerk, he looked at Todd with a strange mixture of respect and wonder.

When he opened the box on the table, a royal purple velvet cloth spilled out. There was something with a dirty, dusty brownish hue that fit in the box with perfect accuracy, despite it being a rounded shape, almost like the box was made for it. Todd's heart beat faster—he knew what the dirty round thing was. Hamok held the box out to him and Todd's creeping suspicion was proven horribly right: it was a skull.

Todd recoiled. "Jesus, man—"

Darting his gaze between the box's contents and the

now-somber face of the older man holding it out to him, it was on the second glance back at the skull that Todd realized something didn't fit right with the picture.

The skull inside the box wasn't...completely...human. The curve of the scalp and forehead along with the hollow eye sockets were slightly larger for a human being, while the nasal cavity appeared a bit bigger than normal too, wider. The jaw was above average size as well, but nothing elongated or extreme. But it was past the jaw and the teeth inside that stopped everything in Todd.

It was the teeth.

The incredibly sharp teeth.

"What...*is* that?" Todd knew it wasn't fake or a plastic mold in any way. It was authentic in *every* way, which was probably why Todd felt his body temperature drop in the humid house. This was real. Everything in Todd's reserve of instinct told him it was.

"Well, it's certainly not something you see every day, as the American saying goes."

"Certainly," Todd said, still staring.

"This was *my* calling, young friend." Hamok set the box on the desk in front of Todd, then fell back into his rolling desk chair. "If the sea wills it, it will happen, as it has happened to you."

"Okay!" Todd threw his hands up in defeat. "Story time. Spill it." Todd moved to the other side of the desk and crossed his arms. "I'll shut up."

Hamok smiled that wide, wild grin again, proud and beaming. "New ones always do, eventually. I'll ask you again: do you want some coffee?"

"Yeah," Todd considered. "I think I do. But if you tell me you have Aquaman on speed dial, I'm gonna beat feet."

Ignoring him, Hamok walked around the desk and out of the office—but not before handing the coin back to Todd, where he returned it to his shirt pocket.

*

Even though it was pushing ten o'clock in the morning, Hamok offered a little kick in the coffee he was brewing for Todd. Todd thought he could use the kick *sans* coffee, but then knew it was still a long drive to Miami and didn't want to take the chance on an empty stomach. Todd asked for only a pinch, out of respect.

With Todd back on the couch in the living room and brewed coffee masking the porky air of his house, Hamok brought him a steaming cup and a package of shortbread cookies. Then he began his story.

"When I was much a younger man, much younger than you, in fact, and nearing puberty, I already had a deep understanding of the lost continent. It was in nearly every part of my life, like a religion. I am Armenian, so normally a deep faith in Catholicism was expected, but not in my family. My father, like my grandfather, was obsessed with finding the answers to where the pieces fit in this grand puzzle."

Hamok reached his weathered recliner and slowly backed-up against it, waddled his backside to the seat as if aiming his butt to the cushion, then just trust-fell back into it with a great sigh, relishing the relief of being off his feet. As he settled, the recliner squealed under his weight; Hamok had to take a couple of breaths before continuing.

"Research at the library was my version of church, going weekly and sometimes daily if they were up for it, if my grandfather's poor knees weren't enflamed. Dusty books and oceanic graphs were my Bible. Looking for the right direction, picking up clues and hints as to where it might lead. My father and grandfather were the learned men I would draw from. I made a friend at the library that let me in on who else was checking out the same books as we were. In time, I found there were other people who shared my family's interests and mine in the Lost Continent, drawn to the mystery, which only fueled the fire. My grandfather would have been so proud of me, had he lived, God rest his soul.

"Anyway, at the time we were living in Miami, naturally, being so focused and always on the verge of a breakthrough. We moved there when I was eleven, picking up all we had and leaving for the states after grandfather passed. And you know what? An amazing thing happened. They *found* us!

"The Society." Hamok stole a sip of coffee before continuing.

"The Society had already started here in Miami and the Keys and they welcomed us with open arms! This was…sixty-some years ago? Seventy, almost? But the Society had already been established before and were doing the same as we were back home right here in the region, checking on the other users of the same books, finding people of the same interests, enthusiasts drawn to the calling. They were wary of us at first, but once we showed them that skull in my office that my grandfather had found all those decades ago, when the sea had chosen our family during a fishing trip in Bermuda, we were invited to share in the same secrets they had gathered. The same knowledge. The same findings. The Bagbarsarians made great gains the day we moved here to South Florida. Even more when we found the Society."

Hamok sat back in the easy chair, his coffee steaming on the end table, becoming lost in the memories. He cleared his throat and rubbed his hands together before continuing.

"And the Society was so much more advanced than what three generations of Bagbarsarian men could have done, but they were impressed, nevertheless. The skull was the invitation for us. It was the proof, the confirmation, and they knew it. The skull was what had my father and I meeting some rather bohemian people in the Society scattered throughout South Florida, even in Cuba and in the Caribbean Islands, and as far east as Naples, Fort Myers, even Sarasota. They had come from all different parts of the world, 'hearing the call', as we like to say."

"As the saying goes," Todd interjected.

Hamok smiled like a pleased parent. "Yes, indeed. With us joining the Society came meetings and organization, a deeper understanding of what we were being told. The acts and faith of many believers can do so much more that just a small family. Collectively, with all the information we had gathered, even with old sea stories and simple rumors taken as clues, we examined and came up with divisions that designated different people who were connected to the various facets of the ultimate find, like Seekers.

"Every time we thought we were about to strike the prize of discovering the Lost Continent, something threw a wrench in the plan. Of course, when your plan of attack is a five hundred-mile triangular battleground that is covered in ocean and known for strange, peculiar things...well, you can get derailed fairly easy. There were lives lost over the years. Many were injured over the decades, physically, emotionally...families were broken up over the search. It was a sad time in my early twenties, but every trip out there we would return with a little more knowledge, a little more experience. Something more to drive us back and make us stronger in our faith.

"Over time, as I grew older, we realized there were rankings to the people involved in this whole thing, in the Society, that we could identify from their...let's call them *abilities*. And from how they were chosen for those abilities. The more we knew, the more we saw the obvious, the more we thought there was a reason why Atlantis was lost to begin with. And that was when we grasped that maybe we were searching for something that, perhaps, should not only *stay* lost, but be protected from ever being found. Something that needed to be out of the general consciousness of the world.

"It was that skull that told us, *my* family. It was some of the other odd and horrible findings that we in the Society came up with—evidence, clues, links—to the whole shebang. How far along, technologically speaking, were the people of Atlantis when that terrible day and night of destruction happened? What kind of technology did they have access to and how did they use it? Did they bring it upon themselves or was there an outside force? Was it even tech, or was it something else entirely? Questions, questions, questions.

"So, to clear your mind, Todd, we do not hide what we know for the Atlantians or Atlantis herself. We hide these truths because we don't want to repeat their destruction. But some don't see it like that. They want the information we have, and how to find the answers to the kind of power we've been gifted. They had their army, oh yes. With the kind of power they had access to, you would think that they would be left alone, which they were. No one ever invaded them, no Great Atlantian War took them down. Some legends speak of opposing foreign armies believing they were fighting actual demons. The truth was, they were fighting something they couldn't comprehend."

This was the only time Todd interrupted Hamok with a question. He was starting to understand and, somewhat, connect the dots. A part of him, maybe, even believed it, which is why he asked, "You mean the skull?"

"Exactly!" Hamok said, as another one of his boney fingers pointed at him.

"Wait a minute. Are you saying they...*created* those things?"

"Yes!" Hamok exclaimed. "They had the kind of intelligence and technology and advantages that we're just now tapping into with genetic manipulation, communications, and cloning. That is how far advanced they were as a civilization. That was why no one ever tried to invade. Why they have gone through the consciousness of humanity as a legend, quivering the spines of any army who dared to defy it, or any dreamer who dared conceive it, because it was all too much for the world to take at that time.

Mercy, some people today can't even handle the power scientists have unlocked with stem cell research and cloning. They protest and scream that it's going to be the end of us. Some of these Seekers, they want this information that we've worked so hard to protect...I mean, the government of nearly every country in the world would want this, not to mention arms dealers, pirates, kingpins, drug lords. Anyone who knows what this is and the kind of power it holds? All of them would come like snarling dogs to create such an army. Think about it. The families of soldiers would never have to mourn a lost loved one because of a war."

That sent shivers under Todd's skin of a certain kind that he hadn't felt in a long time. He was thinking of Kyle, obviously, but also that young soldier that had come to his door in uniform to notify him of his son's death. The way his face looked when Todd had nearly attacked him, when all he had tried to do was comfort the grieving father in front of him. As long ago as Kyle's death was, he briefly wondered if that soldier was even still alive.

"But what they don't consider," Hamok continued, "are the repercussions for such actions. Such as what happened in Atlantis. No one is exactly certain of how it happened, but we have an idea, and it's directly connected with those beasts they created. That skull. But isn't that how it usually goes? When no one can take you down, the best thing to do is wait for you to stumble and cause your own fall. 'Too big to fail', as the American saying goes."

Todd was still thinking about the possibility of future soldiers, millions of young men and women never having to see combat, and the thought of generations to come never having to experience the aftereffects of war. Todd felt his anger rise, a heated and authentic kind, the kind that had boiled to an overflow when he had jumped at the young soldier at his front door. The kind he felt as he watched his son lowered into the ground.

"Hold on," Todd said. "You're telling me that this kind of

technology is possible and out there somewhere and it's a secret that you and your…group…have *kept* from the world?"

"No, Todd. We don't have all the answers. In fact, there are times when I, myself, question my own understanding of this whole thing, and I'm third generation! The religious would call that a lack of faith. But, like I said, we have some…abilities…that reassure us we are on to something greater than ourselves. If anything else, this coin is a major component of *how* to find it. And now that you have it, we can find the information to destroy it. Or, maybe, try to understand it."

"Destroy it? Why the *hell* would we want to do something like that? Something that would save millions of lives?"

"While probably killing *billions* more in the process? Any one man could unlock a deluge of power unto himself. Todd, look at what happened to Atlantis. Where are they now? From what we have gathered, it wasn't a flood or a comet from the sky. It was *upheaval*. From within. The soldiers, their legion of beasts, their *own army,* turned on their designers and creators. We have to look to the past to learn for the future, and if we don't look at the Atlantians as an example, the world is doomed to share the same fate, but on a much grander, much more *permanent* scale."

That statement appeased Todd's anger, but the situation still didn't sit well with him, nor did the sanity of this whole thing. *Was* the skull real? Was Hamok a raving loon that he completely misjudged? Todd rubbed his forehead again, "I can't believe I'm even having this conversation."

Just then, Bermuda jumped back onto the couch next to him, looking at him quizzically, offering a soft meow.

"You have to understand, Todd, that we know more than you think, but we don't know everything. Which is why Alex sent you to me, to tell you of Council."

"Who are they?"

"They are the appointed leaders of the Society. And you will need to meet with them soon. You'll want to."

"What do you mean?" Todd had started stroking Bermuda's back once more without realizing it, and finding it therapeutic. It was something to keep his hands busy, to calm him down, keep control.

"It's just what I said: we don't know everything. We're not completely sure how any of this exists, or where Atlantis would even be," Hamok explained, and Todd caught the regret teeming in his voice. "But nearly every one of us in the Society has evidence in one way or another. Still, there isn't even enough proof that they exist. Here, anyway."

"I'm not following you."

"These...*occurrences*...findings...that have been recorded in the Triangle, we think they have been reaching out to us from Atlantis, trying to communicate. They—"

Todd held up his opened hand. "Wait, what? You think Atlantis is still around? Still alive?"

Hamok only looked at him. "We don't know everything yet."

"Look, I only know a little bit about the place, but I *know* that it's gone, and that's if it even existed at all. That was thousands of years ago. *Thousands*. Don't play me for dumb, okay? Come on."

"I don't believe that you are. You believed enough to come up here. You believed enough to stick around and hear my story and see my artifacts. You must have some crumb of faith inside you."

"Faith is that overused word when small-minded people need convincing. This isn't some geek sci-fi fantasy. This is me losing a day of painting, not selling any art, and wasting my time. Besides, there are huge holes in your story. You know that, right? If you're not completely sure, then how can you be so sure? On top of that, where is your proof they're still alive?"

Hamok said, "Because, we've devised a prophecy and we see the signs. And soon enough, you will too."

Todd thought that sounded like a mixture of a loaded response and a bunch of baloney. "A prophecy? Really? Are we getting that clichéd here?"

"There is enough evidence for us to believe there is one," Hamok said. "We feel it, as a whole, as a unified Society. But it isn't the Seekers that are the most obvious and the most dangerous you will encounter. People will want this coin, trust me. They're just the beginning of your cha—"

Hamok was cut off as Todd's cell phone rang in his pocket with a loud, jolting chatter. Hamok stopped and had the expression of a man who had never heard a cell phone before, as if the device were completely alien to him. Just before Todd answered, though, he thought he looked as if he was morbidly expecting the call.

The digital display face said "Mark". Todd figured he'd gotten the note and was just worried about the sudden departure.

"Hello?"

The first things Todd heard were a rush of voices and sirens in the background—hardly what he expected.

"Todd? *Todd?*" It was Mark alright, and he was frantic.

"Yeah, Mark, it's me, what—"

"Where are you, man? Are you okay?"

"I'm at a friend's house. What's going on?"

"The shop, man. Something happened to your studio. Somebody shot it up."

Todd stopped breathing.

In fact, his whole body went cold.

He didn't know what to say to that. He didn't know how to feel, either. "*What?*"

"Glass is *everywhere*. Man, your art…Todd, it's completely destroyed. All your canvases are shot up. Your work is gone, man. *Gone!* It was a drive-by. I'm-I'm so sorry. Your prints, the door, the glass. It's all shot up. Your studio is a mess."

"What about you? Are *you* okay, Mark?"

"Yeah, I dove behind the counter when it started." Mark was on the verge of tears. "I tried to get a plate number. I really did, but they took off before I could get it. I think, I think they're in a gang because they vandalized your place too. They sprayed a big red triangle on your wall and on my car before they left."

If the call itself froze him, that comment stopped Todd Freeman's heart. "They did what?"

"They drew a—" There was another voice in the background that interrupted him. The authority of it indicated to Todd that it was perhaps a fire marshal or a police officer. "I gotta go, man. The cops are here. Please call me soon."

"Let me know—"

But Mark had hung up.

Todd had been looking at the cat during the whole call, but not really. He saw Mark, and his studio, his *life*, in tatters and full of bullets. When he closed his phone, he looked over at Hamok, who had leaned back in the chair, arms crossed, and was staring at him.

"They're already tracking you," he said. "They know where you're at."

"*How? How* did they know?"

"Where do you live, friend? This is a chain of islands, Todd, and when something is found that is of importance, people hear about it in a hurry, one way or another. You think I don't know who you are? Selfless Scavenger? Local artist? Your face is known here, not just for your art but your generosity too, which is going to work against you the longer you're down here. My guess is that Alex insisted you get to the city, correct? There was a reason for that. In Miami, you can hide, blend in, and get to Alex, who can take you to Council. It's bigger, and harder for them to find you. But don't think that you are alone. The Society is here to help.

There are people on your side that are stationed throughout the Keys and even in Miami. Go to Alex. Don't go back to your gallery; there's nothing there that can help you now."

Hamok made another grand struggle to the edge of his recliner and forced himself to his feet. After a couple of steps, he gestured for Todd to follow him back into the office again. This time both he and Bermuda followed him.

Hamok found a pad of paper on his cluttered desk and, miraculously, a pen right next to it. He began scribbling. Bermuda soon joined him on the desk, meowed again, and turned its attention to the window. "This is my number. I will be here. Remember, you have reinforcements. Don't be scared to use them. They're on your side." Hamok handed the folded scrap over to Todd but looked past him and then down at the floor between them, as if he didn't want to make eye contact, as if he was figuring out how to say goodbye to a close friend instead of someone he'd just met.

After a pause, Todd took the paper and Hamok continued. "Look, I am deeply sorry for your loss, for your place. If I know who you are, then they definitely know who you are." Hamok's eyes slowly rose and found Todd's. "You had good reason for coming here and you were smart enough to trust your instincts. I'm sorry you feel like you were tricked into coming. I assure you, there were no tricks. You made a leap of faith to trust Alex's warnings and that took balls. I hope with what I've shown you here," Hamok waved a hand at the box holding the not-so-human skull, the maps and layouts in abundance in and around the office, "and what your phone call has told you, that you will continue on to Miami, to trust the process, as the saying goes."

Todd didn't know how to answer him in that short and fleeting moment. He probably would have just leaned on the reality that he had a mess waiting for him back home that was looking more and more connected to the coin in his pocket.

But just as he was about to open his mouth again, Bermuda

started hissing, canines exposed as the cat faced the westside window—the one looking out onto the street.

At this, Hamok eyes grew wide in terror. "Oh, shit. They're already here."

Then it happened.

CHAPTER 8

ATTACK

WHEN HAMOK FIRST pushed him out of his way, Todd was taken aback by the force of this older, bonier frame against his, particularly for a man who creaked and popped with nearly every movement.

"Who's here? The same people who shot up my place?"

Hamok didn't answer. Instead, he scrambled out of the office so fast for an old man who'd for the last hour moved at the speed of tree growth that Todd could only marvel at it.

By the time Todd reached the doorway of the office, a mere four paces behind the old man, his open-mouthed marveling quickly transformed into shocked amazement, as he bore witness to the first of the many other incredible things Hamok Bagbarsarian could apparently do.

In one long, fluid movement, Hamok dove over the messy coffee table and snatched the giant bejeweled blade. Or did he just see the knife...what? Jump into his hand? On its own? Or was the old man just that quick? Either way, "graceful" couldn't begin to describe the supernatural agility—especially when Hamok landed on the couch, twisted his body and launched the blade right at the door just as a man burst inside, the blade sinking deep into the invader's chest.

The man trembled. Gasped. Choked.

This huge, uninvited guest, dressed in black fatigues and whose size could have made him a professional linebacker, cried out with a final grunt and dropped the Uzi in his hand.

It was the first time Todd had ever seen someone die in real life right in front of him. Or laid eyes on an actual Uzi, for that matter.

Hamok jumped to his feet from the couch, speedy and fleet. Still stunned, Todd could only watch. He had entered a whole new reality from just ten minutes ago. Hell, ten *seconds* ago.

"Come on," Hamok said to him, crossing his living room and going for the Uzi and the blade.

"*What?*" Todd suddenly realized his knees were weak, the energy to stand nearly depleted as he had to lean against the wall for support. Everything was happening too fast. Even his voice sounded shaky as he watched Hamok snatch the Uzi and yank the blood-streaked blade from the man's chest, as squishy, juicy blood noises reaching Todd's ears.

Holy shit, this is happening.

Somehow, Todd found the strength to move toward the front door only to be met with Uzi-fire erupting outside. Bracing, throwing his arms over his face, he fell on his ass at the unexpected loudness of it. A short peek at the doorway brought the sight of Hamok going full-blown Rambo on the house's front porch, spraying bullets, and screaming.

In any other instance, say in a movie or some eccentric television comedy, Todd would have found it funny to see a seventy-plus-year-old man on the front porch of his house, battle-crying at the top of his lungs with roaring artillery and his whole body shaking from the jolting power of the weapon. The whole scene was so outlandish that to see it play out in front of him and not in that movie or on a bizarre television show was beyond surreal. In this instance of real life, however, on the dirty carpet that smelled like old coffee and bacon grease, inches from a dead body that stared at him with unmoving hazel eyes with his own hand raised pathetically in front of his face, not even a smirk found his lips.

"*Come on*," Hamok screamed again, after a short pause in the firing. That beat was just quick enough for the command, but just short enough for the enemy (one Todd still didn't see, other than the dead body on the floor) to return fire two-fold. Hamok ducked as splinters of wood shot out of the doorway and porch, launching them in every direction while the sound of his descent on the steps creaked inside the house, even with the distant gunfire. Todd curled up as he heard Hamok scream and fire back.

Pop-pop-pop-pop!

Todd looked up from the floor as the sound of the gunfire moved away from the door of the house and into the street, echoing through the green canopy in a firecracker cacophony. As he stole his peek, Bermuda the fat tabby scurried out from the back of the house and, to Todd's complete and brief surprise, out into the paved battlefield with Hamok.

Todd was about to get to his feet and (unbelievably) follow Bermuda into the warzone when the whole house rocked to the left and took a short jolting slump downward. Todd sprawled back on his knees and fell to his open palms. He was only on the floor for a second before remembering the house's already rickety and unstable-looking stilts, and that the gunfire was most likely aimed at one of those aged wooden posts. How many were there? Five? Six? He knew when he first showed up it wouldn't take much to literally bring the house down. Apparently, so did the people shooting at them.

Todd climbed back to his feet a second time and was only permitted a few pithy seconds to think of his next move.

Before he could act, the large curtained window shattered, unleashing a diamond storm of glass over the couch and coffee table in front of it. On the opposite side of the house, the first massive crack shot up and around the front door where Hamok had been standing not a moment before. With the window destroyed, a twin crack about the width of Todd's arm shot up through the wall and over the ceiling, looking like black lightning etched onto it. It only took a few blindingly fast seconds for the cracks on either side to meet just above Todd's head as dust and drywall snowed down to the floor. The enemy had started it. Gravity was about to finish it.

With a cataclysmic crack of the support beams and an explosive split of the house's aged structure, the whole southern half of Hamok's house—a section of the living room, a spare bathroom Todd had spotted and, of course, Hamok's shrine of research and devotion to his quest—came down like a playset destroyed by a tantrumming child, the stilts chewed away by gunfire.

Plumes of dust and debris shot into the air, and geysers of papers and chunks of drywall were blown in every direction. Chaos touched every corner and item in the house, all the minor props of Hamok's life sent flying and shattering. His office collapsed to the ground, his decades of research and obsession, gone in a matter of seconds. The television that had been mercifully hushed at Todd's arrival was silenced forever as it spilled over in the cascade of the home and landed face down, the glass tube shattering. The house vomited over into the street, a mess of waste and loss.

Todd dove toward the small dinner table on the other side of the kitchen as half the house came down, thinking in that short span of seconds he was doing a poor imitation of Hamok's ability to leap into the air like some otherworldly geriatric Parkour expert. Miraculously, the table was still standing with the chairs neatly pushed up to its edges, unaffected by the destruction around it. This defensive effort wasn't but a second in time, as the crumbling half of the house plummeted to the ground, sending a huge cloud of dust and debris into the muggy, morning air.

After landing on the floor (again!) and hearing a few bullets wiz by just over his head, along with the thumping, distant ache in his knee from the last fall, Todd suddenly recognized this was his only chance at surviving. The rising cloud of the collapsed house was already thinning but it was still a distinct, albeit temporary, wall blocking any view of the enemy and presumably, any view of him.

Pop-pop-pop-pop-pop!

Hamok was still calling him, screaming his name, his voice magnified now, as was the Uzi fire, with half the house cracked open like a melon. He had to act.

Crawling toward the short cliff of Hamok's ravaged house, Todd found the main horizontal support beam of the structure broken in half and jutting into the rising dust. Todd knew he was going to use this main post when he first saw it, and as he reached it and began climbing across from the open edge of the house, still near to the floor, he tried to peek at the street. Todd thought he spotted a black car through the dust and gun smoke. Three of the four doors were open, and a few armed men hid behind the hideous crackle of their arsenal.

More bullets. More shots. More yelling from Hamok. The insanity of this whole thing was pressing toward all out war.

What in fuck's name had that stupid coin gotten him into?

Though his blessings were coming in small doses this morning, Todd received another one when he looked down to see Hamok's mattress, half-unclothed from the spill with a comforter and sheets ripped from it. Taking aim from the broken support beam, he jumped from the edge of the living room down to the mattress, this time aware that he should land on the *other* knee.

As he fell, a micro-morbid thought passed through his mind of a broken spear of wood jutting upward just behind the mattress, a trap that would burst through the coils, pierce the flimsy padding, and gore him.

But that didn't happen. Instead, he thought he could have mimicked a safety video about tumbling and rolling from fires (or in his case, collapsing houses). His other knee didn't collide with any other hard or sharp objects beneath it, and after he had barrel-rolled onto the house's oil-stained concrete base, he thought the whole action was probably the smoothest thing to happen to him today.

Todd knew it was the adrenaline of the gunfire and the yelling, but once he reached ground level, the pain in his knee subsided even more, allowing him to clamber to his feet. The collapsed rubble of the house and the plumes of dust clouds had become Todd's best defense, a smokescreen of fortification.

"Todd!" Hamok screamed again. His voice was much closer now and easier to find. Todd reacted to the call and ran around the barrels and collected storage that Hamok had been using as a shield.

Hamok's back was against the rusted oil barrels as sweat coursed down his face, but thankfully and amazingly, he hadn't been hit or even scraped by a bullet. In fact, Hamok did one better and had a second Uzi in his other hand, both weapons currently smoking.

"What do you want me to do?!" Todd, frantic beyond any other point in his life, had to scream it over the gun blasts and their echoes.

"Cover me!" Hamok shoved one of the Uzis into his hand. Todd stiffened, thought he could have blurted out a *"Wait"* or a *"Hold on,"* but he wasn't able. Hamok was off. He was familiar with a handgun, and even then, it had been years, but an Uzi?

With Hamok's departure, the gunfire started up again and Hamok dutifully returned it. Todd could only duck in reaction, missing his opportunity to argue against the old man's quick-thinking proposal.

By the time he was able to look up again, Hamok had already maneuvered from the oil barrels, crates, and boxes that were near his Cadillac to the secured and covered wall formed by the wreckage of his house, roughly ten feet away from Todd. Of course, with the battlefield being nothing but a quiet island street and the enemy closing in, ten feet was a deathtrap.

Somehow and at some point during his fight, Hamok had acquired a long thick chain and was swiftly fastening it to the bottom of the bejeweled hilt of the knife that had been stuffed between his belt and his linen shorts. The blood of the first fallen intruder had dribbled over some of its sparkle, but as Hamok connected the long blade to the chain, the handle still glistened in the partial sunlight. Enough so that Todd never questioned what he planned to do after Hamok connected the chain and knife together.

Hamok turned to him from that distance with a disbelieving look. "Todd! What are you doing? Get over here! Move! Cover me!"

Todd snapped out of his observation and attempted to join Hamok, his finger placed delicately on the trigger. Then, he pointed the gun in the direction of the oncoming bullets and pulled the trigger of his Uzi, sprinting the ten-foot gap. He only got off a few rounds in its noisy, bone-vibrating clatter in his hand, but he did make it across without dying or getting a bullet or five to the ribs. Though, some of the enemy fire knocked a few crates over and ricocheted off the oil barrels in a couple of *pling-ploon* sounds, Todd jerking away from the oncoming fire.

As he approached, Todd had to shout over the gunfire again, but he couldn't hold back any longer, exploding on Hamok, "*How* are you doing *any* of this?!"

Hamok ignored him and instructed Todd to take the other Uzi sitting on the oil barrel, which he did. Now he was the one double fisting it Rambo-style in this crazy battle. To say he did not see his day going this way would be the understatement of the century.

Hamok let the knife slip from his hand and dangle, gripping the chain and giving it a little slack. The chain was a good ten feet in length, probably more, and Hamok tightened his grip on it. His wrinkled, liver-spotted hands looked misplaced by the embattled and expectant warrior stance he was now taking. Hamok checked the other side of the fallen home to see if any of the gunmen were coming from that side. Then, facing the direction of the gunfire, he spoke.

"All right. There's two more left. They're going to come in hard. We have to go in together. I'm going to blitz it in three seconds—I need you to cover me while I go in. All I ask is that you don't shoot me." Then Hamok looked back over his shoulder. "You got that?"

"Three? I can't—"

"Two seconds."

"*Hold on!*"

"Go!"

Hamok rushed around the rubble of his house with the same uncanny, animal agility he'd displayed just a few traumatizing moments ago, only this time at full tilt and out in the open.

He ran slightly bent, charging the open street with a trained assassin's covertness and precision. The other interesting thing Todd happened to catch before moving himself: Hamok was swinging the chain and the blade on the end of it, like a lasso.

Just before Todd rounded the ruins of Hamok's house and into the wide open where the Uzi-armed enemy awaited them, he thought, with a mixture of despair, desperation, and raging fear, *This goddamned coin better be worth it.*

*

Hamok kicked ass.

The old dog did nothing more or less, moving with that same unbelievable smoothness and deadly accuracy that sailed past mere human ability and deep into realms of the impossible. That was what Todd caught, anyway, in the short quick glances that he was allowed during this short and completely insane blitz.

Hamok fought with less gymnast in his movements this time

and more charging headlong ninja. Right from the start, even with Todd's choppy views and distracted focus on the other attackers—not to mention brandishing two Uzis for the first time in his life—Todd could see the uncanny swiftness in the way Hamok moved. It was extraordinary not just for a seventy-year old card carrying AARP member, but for a *human man*, period.

After Hamok took off around the corner through the settling dust of his ruined home and Todd reluctantly followed, he was finally given a real view of what he was up against. The flying bullets and the swift and sudden destruction of the house painted in Todd's mind a vision of some small, devoted army awaiting them, with proper artillery to match. Given the black fatigues, too, it had to be some organized squadron.

But when Todd rounded the fallen corner of Hamok's house, he finally saw the enemy and found not a SWAT-like team but more a mafia-style mix of covertness, sleekness, and bang-up suits—all with a colorful splash of Caribbean flair. At one point during the blazing insanity that followed, Todd thought they looked like pimps from Antigua or St. Barts.

The first time Todd pulled the triggers of the Uzis in this rush, he considered he actually *did* shoot Hamok in the process, the guns going off with that same shocking sputter in every possible direction. To say he felt emasculated in those frighteningly brief seconds would be an understatement of a lifetime, too. To add insult to injury, the old man's speedy movements dodged everything Todd and the tropical insurgents might have accidentally or purposefully hurtled his way. Todd used his juvenile handling of the Uzis, as well as the bluntness of them, mainly as an amateur diversion that luckily *did* hit the open doors of the enemy vehicle, where they were crouched in defense.

What Hamok did, the way he did it, and his fighting prowess, confirmed to Todd his role immediately: nothing more than that presumed noisy distraction. Because when Hamok rounded the corner at full tilt, still swinging the blade in a loop at his side, Todd didn't think they even saw the speedy geriatric until it was too late. Their focus was on Todd's spewing Uzis and ducking from his hail of misdirected bullets.

The two remaining gunman, one who wore a white panama hat and aviators, and the other in a bright turquoise durag, also sporting aviators, had crouched behind the driver and passenger doors, respectively, once Todd started firing.

They were right where Hamok needed them to be.

In his warrior's charge forward, Hamok reached the grill of the luxury car and leapt in one graceful bounce off the side of the black Mercedes' front driver's side tire and onto its open door, slamming it into the driver and pinning the big man before launching the blade across his hefty throat on the bounce back to the pavement. The driver in the white panama hat, who's neck was as thick as a tree trunk sprouting from a tropical Hawaiian shirt, split open in a grand spray of crimson. Clutching at his newly torn flesh, the driver dropped the .44 he was clutching and reached for his neck. In these short seconds the gunfire had paused, Todd could hear the gurgled gasping of the fat driver as he tumbled to the ground, clutching his torn throat, his hat falling next to him and soaking up the blood quickly pooling there.

In the span of a few fleeting seconds, and after a stunning display of ancient warrior-style combat mixed with the smoothness and training of a skilled trapeze artist, Hamok's visual display caused the final death surges of the driver to be lost in his otherworldly performance.

Because before the husky man even hit the ground, Hamok leapt over the driver's side door in a tumbling back flip, caught the falling pistol, landed in a crouched position on one of his knees as if proposing, aimed, and shot through the glass of the Mercedes, striking the other durag-sporting gunman on the other side. Durag collapsed to the ground, his head partially held up by the car door, his body sporadically twitching from the sudden kill. Hamok remained on his knee, holding the smoking gun outward.

Todd lowered the Uzis and could only blink in reaction.

As the gunfire echoed through the canopy for the last time, Todd only stood there, utterly stunned, as Hamok did the most incredible act yet. A showstopper to end all showstoppers.

Bouncing to his feet, the old man returned to that warrior-Kung-fu-master's stance of concentration, looking at the car directly before him. Then, with his opened palms and splayed fingers raised and directed toward the vehicle, chain and blade dangling over the crook of one elbow, Hamok—without touching the Mercedes—*lifted* the vehicle off the ground.

Glass tinkled from the shattered windshield. The car groaned as it came off the leaf and shell casing littered pavement. It wasn't until the huge Mercedes had risen at least two feet off the ground that Todd noticed the two dead gunmen were being lifted into the air as well. The aviators fell off Durag's face while the driver's throat continued to pump blood down his now-soaked Hawaiian shirt.

They were merely floating in the air next to Hamok, suspended by nothing.

Whatever force or power Hamok possessed, it was on full display today for Todd to witness. Of course, all of this—the guns blazing, Hamok's bizarre mysticism, and now, this incredible mastery over objects he wasn't even touching—was so well beyond Todd's sphere of understanding as to break the outer reaches of his reality, very nearly shattering his sanity. Todd didn't have a logical, rational explanation for the past ten minutes. The gymnastics, the gunplay, his *uncanny* speed, and martial arts fighting was surreal, yes, even ethereal, but the capability to lift a car without touching it with such dominance over the physically impossible was what made Todd drop the Uzis to the ground in pure amazement. The strength in his arms had turned to hot butter. If the Uzis had gone off, Todd probably wouldn't have noticed. If a couple of rounds had gone off in his foot or shin, he probably would've noticed that, either.

The silence of the street was thunderous now, just like it was when he had first arrived. Even the echo of the gunfire was completely gone. And with Hamok's hands outstretched and steady, levitating a car on his own accord five feet in front of him, brought that suddenly unnerving silence to deafening tones. Even the glass stopped tinkling to the ground. There were only the squeaks and groans of the car's undercarriage and shifting weight.

Holding the car and their ground-level attackers steady, Hamok turned his attention to the front door of his house and the splintered remnants of his still (incredibly) lifted porch. Like a maestro conducting an orchestra, he reached out his other hand dramatically toward it and closed his fist. As Hamok slowly drew his fist closer to his body, Todd watched the original attacker in all black float out the front door as if on an invisible stretcher to rejoin his defeated crew floating in the air in the middle of the street.

To bring home the point that Todd Freeman's life was never going to be the same after today, Hamok remained in that dramatic stance for a moment longer before slowly craning his neck to look at him, eye to eye. Hamok wobbled on his feet, clearly exhausted and spent of energy, but he had wanted to make sure Todd was watching him. And Todd knew it.

Without saying a word, Hamok glared deep into Todd's saucer-sized eyes, where tears were quickly forming at the sight of something so astonishing and unbelievable, something of Biblical authority, or a comic book's fantastical enthusiasm.

In that silence, Hamok only nodded once, a short, tired bob of the head, as if to confirm that, *Yes, Todd. This is also real. Everything you've ever been taught before, everything you've ever believed, isn't what it really is and here is the proof.*

Breaking eye contact and shaking the chain and the blade off the crook of his elbow to the pavement in a loud jingle, Hamok turned his focus back onto the car. His hands were still held before him, looking like they were trying to balance the weight of the vehicle and its deceased passengers hovered above. The insurmountable fatigue in his body language, in just those five steps, as well as in his drooped face, indicated that he was drained. But as if Todd needed any more convincing, Hamok stole the final drop of energy he had left for one more surprise: his biggest yet.

Slowly and with the same careful, ginger motions as when he was stepping down his porch not a hour ago, one foot at a time, Hamok bent to one knee and crouched, stretching the other leg out behind him and putting both of his arms straight out in front of his body—his right outstretched and his left across his chest. He then closed his fists tight enough for veins to protrude, even with his thin and aged skin. Todd thought it was a strange position to be in, but it wasn't until it was too late that he realized who Hamok resembled in the moment: a shot-putter about to heave their stone.

Hamok shut his eyes, took a breath, and with enough exertion to scream, jumped back five paces toward Todd, flinging his arms over his head like he was holding onto an invisible lasso…and then launched the big Mercedes sedan through the canopy of trees, into the blaze of the morning light.

*

Todd hadn't fully understood the meaning of the word 'stunned' until that very moment. Shocked, yes. He knew shocked very well from experience. But stunned to complete immobility, even down to breathing capability, was foreign to him until the moment he watched that black Mercedes flung into the sky in a grand arc all the way to the moment it crashed into the calm gulf waters, threehundred yards out, with an explosive splash thirteen second later.

Broken branches fell around him, as did many, many leaves, all raining down on Todd as he looked up at the new car-sized gap in the canopy. His mouth hung open as wide as the new hole in the street's green ceiling and as he turned to Hamok, shaking on his feet, Todd finally realized he wasn't holding the Uzis any longer. Magically, they were on the ground just in front of him. He hadn't even heard them drop from his hands.

The old man wobbled on his feet, his back arched. He looked like he had just run the Boston Marathon, and his heaving chest only accentuated this. Hamok almost fell back from pure exhaustion, but he caught himself.

That broke Todd's stunned hypnosis, thankfully for Hamok—because the second time he actually did collapse, though Todd had the presence of mind to rush over and catch him.

Hamok fell back into Todd's arms. The heat coming off him was extraordinary, but the force and power in that first push in the office was long gone. In Todd's arms, Hamok was just another frail, glassy-eyed old man once again, out of breath and ready for a nap. Maybe even a dirt nap. The exertion of it all had sucked him of the ability to stand—and, from the look on his face as Todd lowered him to the pavement, to go on living.

Hamok continued to breath in heavy gasps and Todd didn't know what to say. His only comfort was a quick reminder that he didn't think *anyone* would have known what to say either. Not after the attack—not after that kind of display of inhuman *power*. Todd grasped for words as he cradled Hamok's head, and just when Todd thought Hamok was going to pass out from hyperventilating, his breathing slightly slowed and the glassy look in his eyes began to clear. With it, Hamok blinked and turned his head, his eyes meeting Todd's, which must have been the size of tennis balls with his leaking tears.

A small grin broke over Hamok's mouth, seeing the amazement written all over Todd's face. In a raspy voice a tread above a whisper, he said, "Now…do you…believe me?"

Todd's breath caught in his throat again but was released with a bark of laughter, a high-pitched, insane laugh that Todd couldn't recognize as his own. It almost sounded happy.

The laugh died as Hamok creakily—though successfully—sat up. He shook his head, pressed his palm to his temple as if fighting a headache. He shut his eyes against whatever pain he was feeling and, as if on queue, there came the distant, soul-sinking wail of sirens, growing closer.

Both Hamok and Todd glanced to the end of the street, which was still empty for the time being, and then back at each other. Hamok only needed to look at him for Todd to know he needed to get out of Isla De Oro and to Miami as soon as he could.

"Go, son," Hamok gasped, nodding for him to leave. This was followed by another cough, one strong enough Todd could feel Hamok's stringy muscles tighten through his shirt. At least he wasn't a human furnace anymore. Todd had thought he was going to actually catch fire a moment ago, but his temperature had dropped considerably.

"There's a back alley, over there…" He raised a boney finger and pointed to the short dock that extended into the gulf. The Mercedes was already well below the surface. But it was just before the dock, where the wood planks met the shore, that Todd spotted the small, sandy, overgrown alleyway that ran along the beach. Had Hamok not informed him, he would have thought it was a private driveway, if he'd noticed it at all.

Todd turned back, relieved to have an escape route, but worried about Hamok. "What about you?" The sirens were near.

"I'll be fine. Get to Alex." Hamok tried to roll onto his hands and knees and Todd helped him. "Get out of here, Todd. You don't have much time."

Todd stole only a second more to see if Hamok truly was going to be all right. Then he jumped to his feet and ran for his car.

He hadn't even wondered if his Buick had been shot up in the gun battle. Or if a tire had been blown out, or something even worse. What if the engine was full of bullets? Hamok's ancient Cadillac was half-buried under his collapsed house and had taken the brunt of the destruction.

He pulled out his keys before he reached his covered station wagon and, with them in his hand, knocked the remaining pots that hadn't been blasted to pieces off the hood and ripped the dirty, dusty covering off of the car, silently praying it would start.

Tossing aside the covering, Todd quickly examined his ride with a sinking dread in his stomach. The old Buick had its fair share of bullet holes, mainly near the rear: the back taillight had been shot out, and the rear dome window was completely shattered, as was the driver's side back window.

But...from the looks of it, the tires were still full and didn't appear to be leaking air, and no bullet holes appeared to have penetrated anywhere near the engine, thankfully blocked by Hamok's Cadillac. Todd stooped for a quick glance under the car and didn't see any severe leakage; just the trickle of the typical A/C water.

Jumping in, and no longer praying but pleading to whatever Atlantian God had set him on this screwball trip this morning, Todd held his breath and—yes! Revved up the GM engine. He nearly melted in relief. Maneuvering around a few miscellaneous items from Hamok's destroyed house that had found their way to the driveway, Todd stole another peek at the old man. He had managed to get to his feet, and was still not only clearly exhausted, but in pain too. His back was partially turned to Todd, a hand resting on the lower end of it, but even from his advantage, Todd could see the wince on his face. At least he wasn't wobbling on his feet anymore.

The sirens sounded like they were coming from all directions, forcing him to wonder what he would do if they attempted to sneak through the very alleyway Hamok had suggested.

After he pulled out of his spot among the rubble, Todd threw the big car into drive, squealed tires, and maneuvered his Buick to the canopied alleyway where the smooth pavement curved right and Hamok's island alley became rocky and full of sandy, grassy holes. Miraculously, the alley was clear of any police cars or rifle-ready cops, thinking he was a suspect. Before he escaped the street, Todd paused one final time, still unsure if Hamok would be all right.

Apparently, he was already more than all right. He was hobbling his way down the middle of the street toward the US 1, away from his half-destroyed home. When the first of the approaching fleet of screaming police squad cars turned down the canopied street, he began waving his arms back and forth, flagging them down.

Todd took his queue. Easing onto the gas, he snuck away, slipping through the secret passage.

He barely drove fifty feet down the alleyway when, to his right, he was offered a brief opening in the greenery that looked out onto the warm Atlantic waters of the Gulf Stream of Isle De Oro. He also thought it was looking out on the same spot Hamok had hurled the Mercedes and the three gunmen. As if to confirm the exact location of the sinking car, five vibrantly hued flamingos glided down onto the calm waters and tip-toed their way to a perfect landing, wings sprawled, heading for the sandbar.

It was the first time since he'd moved to Florida that he'd seen wild flamingos. Todd struggled to reassure himself the sight was a good omen.

CHAPTER 9

TO MIAMI

TODD WANTED TO scream.

He'd escaped better than he ever could have believed, but he still wanted to scream. He heard the cops all around him, all sounding like the end of the world in this little community. He was certain his battle-weary Buick was going to be seen, pulled over, and that he would be questioned about the whole gun battle…and then what would he say? The truth? His nerves were completely shot, his mind wouldn't shut off, the adrenaline was still surging, and the realization he had almost died several times in the last twenty minutes was on the verge of being too much for him to handle.

He caught a glimpse of himself in the rearview mirror and gazed at paranoia personified and thought his eyes were ready to truly pop from his head they were so big. Not to mention his skin was a glaze of sweat and dirt, his hair was a mess, at some point he'd gotten a cut on his forehead, and a grey coating of drywall dust (*probably full of asbestos, knowing my luck today*) coated half of his face and down his neck. Then he noticed his, not so anymore, white top shirt and…Jesus Christ…the bullet hole near the bottom left of it that must have just missed him by mere inches.

That shit was real.

For the first time in his life, Todd dry-heaved behind the wheel of a moving vehicle. He let it come, alone in the alleyway, creeping at only fifteen mph, knowing there was only a little bit of coffee in his system, but even that was reluctant to rise. He reached back and snatched an empty paint can from the backseat just in case it changed its mind.

The sirens continued to wail.

Except, he never once actually *saw* a police car until he reached the main highway four streets over. The alleyway had been the most covert route he could've taken, and he would've taken it further but for the alley ending at the fourth street he crossed, giving him no other choice but to turn left toward the main drag. Surprisingly, from Hamok's to the main road he spotted only one other person—an elderly woman. She stood perfectly still outside one of the older stilted homes up the street, her hand on her hip, mouth agape, and staring at Todd over her glasses, deciphering what all the commotion a few streets over was, Todd presumed. She never waved to him, and he never offered one. Todd only hoped she didn't notice his broken back window as he sped on to the main road ahead, a hope he'd cling to all the way up to Miami and with every person he passed.

It was there, at the intersection of US 1 and that random residential side street, that Todd watched two police cars and an unmarked SUV race past him toward Hamok's house, lights twirling, engine revving, and sirens screaming in a warble. Todd waited, letting the parade pass by, trying—hoping—to look as invisible as he could in his bullet-ridden car, and then crept away from the chaos, continuing north up the Overseas Highway. As he did, he realized his hands were still shaking, even as he gripped the wheel.

A weight lifted moving away from Hamok's, though he became aware of a far greater weight, settling on his back.

And it felt like a target.

An ambulance blared past him as he did what any good, law-abiding citizen would have done when he slid to the road's shoulder and paused, waiting for the vehicle to pass. He slipped on his shades for some extra incognito. The ambulance flew by without so much as a pause, as did another two police cars right behind it.

Todd continued onward.

Eventually, the wailing faded away. And Todd, whose hair swirled around his head and whose fingers smelled of gunpowder, could hardly believe it was barely 10:30 in the morning.

He thought, *You ever find anything reeeeealllly big?*

It was then he finally screamed, long and loud.

*

The rest of the trip through the Keys seemed slower and longer than what he remembered, but he tried to chalk it up to his strange combination of high-strung nerves and the breathtaking comprehension of his troubles. There was a scorching urgency in Todd to find more information and a better understanding and some direction in this lunacy. Except, wasn't that what he was doing? Wasn't meeting with Alex part of it, part of the journey to understanding?

Still, the one-lane highway seemed interminable, the horizon all around stretching into a white hot oasis of forever, the tranquil image of a million postcards; yet, everything terrified Todd now—had never been this scared in his life, to put an even finer point on it. He wanted Hamok with him, to help him, and even protect him with his…powers. He didn't know what would be waiting for him along the way or how he would survive if his life depended on protecting a stupid, insignificant coin. Particularly one that brought with it so much inconceivable destruction; it was like a hurricane in his pocket.

There was a long expanse of road around Islamorada and,

just beyond that, where he was caught behind a cement truck that looked like it had come straight out of Fallujah, the driver being extra careful around the slightest curves. Within a few miles there was a long conga line of cars behind it, Todd stuck in the middle and forced to continue at a steady, *maddening* forty miles an hour.

Todd hadn't heard anything from Alex or Mark, which worried him. He remembered Mark had pleaded with him to call him back ASAP about his studio, but goddamn, that wasn't even an hour ago that he called. He did not have it in him to handle that mess right now. He was grateful for the radio silence.

It wasn't until nearly twenty past eleven that Hamok, of all people, phoned him on his cell. The call was short and to the point, curt even. How was he doing? Anything suspicious? He could hear cop-chatter in the background, similar to when Mark had called him.

When Todd had answered both of Hamok's questions positively, Hamok seemed satisfied to ask another, more ambiguous question: if he had caught on to the people watching his back. Todd wasn't sure what he was talking about.

"Start watching the road, Todd. You'll see them."

And with that, he hung up. The call seemed to do nothing but cast over Todd another dark blanket of confusion.

It was about three and a half miles later, though, still moving at that same ungodly slow speed of forty mph behind a pickup truck with a bumper sticker that read *Willie Nelson for President*, that he spotted an older man standing by the side of the road. He wasn't right on the edge, and he wasn't standing near anything particular. There was no mailbox or fruit stand he was manning. He looked like a man waiting at a bus stop. Only Todd hadn't seen any buses all morning; he didn't think a bus route even went through this part of the Keys, and as far as Todd could tell, where the man was standing wasn't even a bus stop. In all probability, anyone passing by would assume him just another old-timer catching a stroll and having a smoke before it got too hot. A cigar smoldered between two fingers, his other hand resting on a cane. He appeared keenly focused on the passing traffic, reminding Todd of those hawk-eyed people on assembly lines who watch for flaws in every manufactured product.

But when Todd approached, the old man's face seemed to shine with something like recognition. Todd thought his own eyes might be playing with him, but he thought he caught a smile from the elderly man, too. Only for him.

Once past, he caught a peek in his rearview mirror of the man's white hair blowing in the breeze, chasing the smoke from his cigar. Seeming satisfied, he slowly turned and watched Todd continue down the road. Just before he disappeared from Todd's view in the side mirror, the old man began walking away from the highway. Todd couldn't tell for sure, but he thought he might have even rambled toward the same woods from which it appeared he'd emerged.

Ten miles later, an almost identical occurrence happened when he spotted another elderly man, standing just off the side of the northbound road. He looked deep in his seventies, though healthy for his age. Standing with his hands behind his back and slightly stooped, he sported a white Van Dyke beard and a black flat cap. Like the man before him, he nodded with satisfaction as Todd passed, then removed himself from the side of the highway, to be lost in shadow.

Seven miles after Van Dyke was a woman, wrinkled, white-haired, the definition of grandmotherly. Eight miles beyond her was an older black man in blue gym shorts and thick-rimmed glasses, standing at his mailbox, a stout little belly stretching his shirt. He actually threw Todd a little wave. Todd couldn't believe he actually threw a wave back. Five miles after him was an older Korean woman who smiled only at Todd when their eyes met.

Each of these elderly citizens stood just far enough away to casually blend in with the background of the passing scene, but close enough to give Todd the sense of some familial oversight. Had Todd not been tuned to notice them, he never would have. He doubted anyone else in the conga line of cars did either.

Even with the temperature on the dash reading a sticky eighty-nine degrees, Todd felt goosebumps break across his arms.

*

About thirty minutes to noon, the heat of the day really struck as Todd reached Key Largo and the due-north section of the Overseas Highway known simply as 'The Stretch'—an eighteen-mile section of road where choppy water and then marsh replaced the solid ground of Key Largo on either side with nary a passing lane to be found. The kind of nightmare traffic that can happen on an extension bridge had been one of the majoring factors why Todd never visited Miami. The constant stop and start couldn't have been good for an aged car like his, either.

So far, however, the Buick had held up pretty well and didn't show any signs of trouble, even with the air conditioning blasting only to immediately blow out the broken back windows. The only problem was the constant line of slow-moving cars in front of him that was his caravanning blockade, making the target he felt earlier now feel illuminated and flashing to everyone he passed. *At least you're still moving, Bucko, and consistently, too. Be grateful for the small wins* he thought, desperately.

He had rid himself of the slow-moving cement truck a few miles back, only to be met with big, blue, concrete dividers closing in on the highway that wouldn't allow him to pass anyone in front of him anyway. Not until he reached the mainland at Florida City, the gateway burg of the Miami metropolitan limits, at the end of The Stretch. Todd's dreaded impossible conga line was here.

Still, suspicion itched him, and the only adequate scratch was keeping his eyes on the cars behind him, and his phone close and plugged into the cigarette lighter.

A few cars crept up the line of slow drivers behind him: a small, red, compact Todd couldn't identify, a black Lincoln, a motorcycle, an orange jeep, and a white SUV. A few glances behind him in the mirror couldn't give Todd a really clear description of the driver of the compact, but he wasn't going to worry unless someone made a move. Especially now that he was on the Stretch: there wasn't going to be much he could do.

About halfway across, right around when the Overseas Highway became South Dixie Highway and where sprawling marsh replaced shallow and choppy ocean water, he realized he hadn't spotted any 'Watchers', the impromptu name he'd given the older folks noticing him pass by the side of the road. Not since the last bait shop at the northern edge of Key Largo—a silver haired Hispanic man with a moustache who shot him a slick up-chin nod of acknowledgement.

Of course, there wasn't anywhere they could fit on the road now and, unless they were hiding in the marsh, Todd was on his own. If anyone was going to attack him, this would be the time. Whether it was going to come from any of these four vehicles or the person on the motorcycle, he didn't know, but he doubted it would come from the small compact.

Todd kept both hands on the wheel, feeling anxious at the sight of the white SUV and the black Lincoln behind him, both formidable competitors to his gargantuan station wagon. Would they really hit him here? Would they have the balls to do it right here, in broad daylight on this bridge, over a coin?

There was that selfsame and continuous line of cars passing on the opposite side of the road, each going by with a quick and rushed *woosh* wind tunnel of sound over the blue median between them. All the Lincoln would have to do is ram the little red compact into him at the right moment and it would send him crashing into the concrete barrier, or worse, over it and into the front of a barreling southbound tractor-trailer. Dramatic, but possible, and that would be the untimely end of Todd Freeman, Chosen One and Protector of the Quarter from Krypton. And that was just assuming it was Lincoln.

The white SUV, how long have they been following me? Or the Jeep? Would *they really do it here?*

Todd knew the answer. Of course they would do it. He also knew it was a stupid question to even ask, a distraction when he was supposed to be keeping his guard up, watching his surroundings for any surprise attacks. They had destroyed Hamok's home in broad daylight with Uzis, after all. What the hell was a public bridge to these people, whoever they were?

How is any *of this possible right now?*

Also: his studio was in ruins. Dear Christ, in *ruins*. What the hell was he going to do? Alex had informed him he would be mutilated if he didn't get out of the Keys, and now he had just met a man who'd told him that the coin he had thought the night before would be a nice base to use on a canvas was actually the keystone to uncovering one of the world's greatest mysteries. Hell, a keystone in proving its existence at all!

It was all so overwhelming. The heat of the day was already reaching intolerable levels, so between it and his anxiety and fear, Todd's whole body was a glaze of sweat. He never thought he would wake up to any of this last night... But neither did he expect to wake up to September 11th either, or that he was going to find out that his son was dead on the other side of the world and being shipped in a body bag back to the States.

He knew he needed to keep calm and do what Hamok told him. What other choice was there? At this point, his curiosity *was* beginning to override his fear. If he really had the protection that Hamok alluded to, with the old-timers guarding over him, he really was protected in some way, right? Especially, if they also possessed something like Hamok's own incredible, inhuman power.

For a little while through The Stretch, he tried to brainstorm how he was going to handle the next few steps. There was nothing but a mess waiting for him back at the studio and he really wasn't in the state of mind to handle that quagmire. Then again, he had his responsibilities he needed to tend to in Key West, his reputation to mend, to begin measuring and evaluating how much work he had lost for the upcoming Christmas season. It wasn't every day that a Selfless Scavenger goes missing only a few hours before his home base goes up in a hail of bullets. And what kind of shit would he catch from the usual authorities on this? He was surprised he hadn't heard a peep from the KWPD.

Still, he continued to press on the gas, one eye on the road, one on the rearview mirror.

Just keep on your toes, Toddy. Just get to Alex's place, get lost in Miami and deal with the studio later. Just watch out for the here and now.

Far in the back of his mind, a question lingered: why would something like this be kept a secret, anyway? That was what puzzled him the most. But then the vision of Hamok hurling the car into the ocean rushed back to him and he realized, no, *that* is what puzzled him the most. And for about the millionth time he considered turning around and giving it all up, even if he was about to hit the mainland, even if his studio was destroyed. What was the point? Why was he even being sent up here to Alex? Why him? How the hell did he get caught up in all this? Because he found this coin? So what? If that was the case, then wasn't he just a messenger for this secret war, this secret quest throughout the islands that not five hours ago he wasn't even aware of?

What had helped Todd in his career with the defense industry was his down-to-earth manner and his critical thinking abilities. Without question, he was the artist and free thinker of the office, and by and large the most creative one of his team, even if it waned in later years, but he still dealt with the world clearly and logically. Reality was reality.

But all this? This was reality, too. And he still had to convince himself of that. This was just an extension of that banal world of spreadsheets and figures and boring shoptalk. Because that world also contained…Atlantis? Weird-skulled monsters with sharp teeth? Old men who could fly through the air and chuck cars like they were empty shoeboxes?

As the Buick rolled on down the highway, he reached the end of The Stretch and the outskirts of tiny Florida City. More cars, and therefore more possible threats, greeted him as he touched his shirt pocket and felt the imprint of the coin.

Just then he passed a sign: 31 miles to Miami.

CHAPTER 10

MAGIC CITY

SOME THINGS NEVER change. Miami was as crowded, balmy, and bright as Todd remembered it being on that initial drive down to his future home on Duval St., over a hundred miles away. Even though the college kids had left for the summer—a nightmare in of itself—it was still a metropolis and hadn't changed from the same circus of retirees, beauty queens, tourists, and muscle men.

He had already started to fight the first sprinklings of outer metro traffic by the time he hit Florida City and the borders of Homestead. Things only got more hectic and crowded as he drove deeper toward the city, through Palmetto Bay and especially so through Pinecrest, as eventually the South Dixie Highway became Interstate-95. The speed and the extra room on the freeway eased his nerves a bit from the stop-start of the smaller villages he'd had to wade though to get here.

Accelerating onto the freeway, Miami's skyline loomed in the distance.

Nearing the high-rise dense Brickell District, where traffic shenanigans started to get really hairy, Alex called him.

"Hey, man. You doing okay?" There was that strange offbeat urgency in his voice he'd heard this morning.

"Oh…" Todd said, trying not to unleash on Alex, "I've been

better, bud. It's noon and I still have my hands, so there's that, but I've been a whole *hell* of a lot better. I mean...what the shit is all this? My place is gon-"

Alex cut him off. "Hey, hey, not over the phone. Okay? We'll talk when you get here. I hadn't heard from you in a while. Status?"

"Just trying to get to you, man. I'm deep in Miami, though. What's up? Black helicopters on my ass now?" He snuck a peek in the rearview mirror, and then out the window to the sky, half expecting them.

"Just stay focused, man. Keep your eyes open, we're not out of the woods yet."

"I'm sure. Traffic's a bitch. This is why I never come up here to see you."

"Has anyone followed you?"

"Not that I'm aware."

"Yes or no, Todd."

He glanced at his rearview mirror again. The black Lincoln that was behind him in Largo and through The Stretch was nowhere to be seen on the crowded highway behind him. Nor was the white SUV, and he'd lost the orange Jeep miles ago.

"No. I don't see anyone."

Sounding satisfied, Alex said "Okay, but don't let your guard down just yet, buddy. How far away are you?"

"Not far. Twenty minutes, from the looks." Todd was admiring the different skyscrapers of Miami cutting into the sky and trying to gauge the distance. "If anything should come up, I'll let you know." Todd said this while looking at the back of a large white delivery truck that had been bouncing along the highway directly in front of him. He had been behind this truck for the past three miles now. He pictured the flimsy clasp of the truck jarring loose over a bump in the road and something heavy and bulky tumbling out, crushing the front of his car. Or worse, the back could always open to another round of Uzis aimed squarely at him.

"Well, if anything *should* come up, don't come here. I know you're close, but you still have—"

"Alex?" Todd said.

"Yeah?"

"I think I might have someone on me." He darted his eyes from the break lights of the truck in front of him to the familiar black Lincoln that was now to his left, just five cars and a semi behind.

"You're serious?" Alex asked.

"It's a black Lincoln."

"How long has he been behind you?"

"Since the beginning of The Stretch, near Key Largo."

"*What?* You said you didn't have anyone tailing you!"

"I thought I lost him a while back. I didn't see him. I'm pretty sure he's following me, though. I could be wrong. It could just be a coincidence." He looked back at the truck in front of him and registered the bright red lights just feet away. He slammed on his brakes. The big car squealed to a halt, his phone almost skittering to the floor as Todd gripped the wheel with both hands.

"What was that? Todd? *Todd?*"

"It's me, that was me, that was my fault, it's okay. I just have to watch the road. I never was one for driving and talking on the phone."

"Where you at?"

"I'm not too far from your exit, maybe a few miles, but traffic looks stopped up ahead. I'm at the Biscayne exit, to downtown, off I-95." Todd glanced at the wrinkled map printout and directions on the passenger's seat, seeing a tangle of converging roads leading into downtown coming up. He had looked at the map several times and knew the directions to Alex pretty well, but didn't want to question his judgment.

Darting his eyes back to the side mirror, he saw the Lincoln was slowly creeping ahead. If they wanted, they could very easily pull up next to him and blow him away right there on the freeway. Or they could just ram him off the side of the road and into the concrete divider. Todd's heart raced as he looked to the road, the rearview mirror, then the side mirror, his left foot tapping nervously.

"Can you get off the ramp now?"

"I should be able too, yeah."

"Take it. Take Biscayne. Then, if he follows, we'll know."

"Okay. Give me a second." Checking his side mirror again and finding the off-shooting lane clear, he pulled the wheel to the far right and eased off the brake. Veering his car around the bumper of the cargo truck, he barely scooted past.

"Okay, I'm getting off of the exit now."

Alex didn't respond.

No other cars followed suit behind him, no mysterious black cars or even any FHP cruisers ready to pull him over for cutting lanes too aggressively. A glimmer of hope.

Either way, no one hindered Todd from the Biscayne Blvd. exit as he rolled over the curved ramp leading to the downtown district, heading due east. Nor, amazingly, was there anyone merging from State Route 970 on his left.

"Todd?" the phone asked.

"Yeah?" As Todd began merging off the interstate, he checked the rearview mirror again.

No one.

Alex asked, "You good?"

Seeing he was about to pierce the heart of downtown Miami, the bright skyscrapers jutting into the equally bright forever-blue above, the lifted Metromover he passed under and eventually the ominously grey Miami Convention Center to his right, Todd believed there might be a chance to lose his pursuer if they actually were tailing him.

Ahead of Todd was the 2nd Ave. cross street, with a traffic light that was currently red. There was only one other car in front of him, a white mid-size Honda that waited at the intersection.

"So far so good."

In front of him, the crossing traffic had slowed to a stop and settled as the red light winked out and changed to green. As it did, Todd wiped the sweat from his face with the back of his arm and stole one final look in the rearview mirror…only to see the black Lincoln barreling down the exit ramp after him.

"Shit!"

"What?"

"He's on to me. He's coming down the ramp right now."

"Shit. What kind of Lincoln is it?" Alex's voice had returned to brusque and demanding. Todd thought he heard paper rustling in the background, followed by the clatter of a keyboard.

"Uh, I think it's a Towncar. I don't know what year. It's one of the newer ones, though."

"Okay, just sit tight. Do you see anything strange about the car?"

"What do you mean?" Todd asked.

"Uh, a license plate that you can't recognize? Maybe a marking on the windshield?"

"Oh, well, I haven't really been looking."

"That's all right. Keep heading straight. And I hate to tell you this, but if you see a red light, you're just gonna have to take it."

"What?!"

"You're just gonna have to trust me on this, okay? In fact, there's one coming up. This is gonna be real quick-like, all right? Like a band-aid or a Tetanus shot. Just go with me on this, okay?"

Todd reluctantly complied, feeling that morsel of hope he had only a moment ago burn away like a scrap of paper in a raging bonfire. He maneuvered the car over 2nd Avenue, wondering what Alex was going to have him do. The one thing on his side was the traffic, which was both (shockingly) light and moving.

As he passed a green-glassed tower, he looked back once more and spotted the Lincoln still following him, only this time there was no one between them. To add insult to injury, Todd heard the Lincoln's engine rev behind him in the cavernous street, attempting to catch up.

The next cross street of SE 3rd Avenue came up faster than Todd expected and, of course, the light was changing to yellow. He was roughly a hundred feet from the crossing street and the Honda that was still in front of him, which was slowly creeping to a stop.

"Alex?"

"Yeah?"

"Alex, the light's turning red."

"Man, take it."

"Do I turn?"

"No, keeping going straight!"

"But—"

"Do it now!"

"Oh shit!" Todd screamed.

In a split second, Todd grit his teeth and wrenched the wheel into the turning lane of SE 3rd Street, pounding his foot on the gas and missing the idling Honda by a yard. Punching his horn and barreling through the intersection like a lunatic on breakout, the wide butt of his huge station wagon fishtailed and bounced over the street. Horns and squealing tires erupted at the corner of 3rd Avenue and 3rd Street as several pedestrians screamed and jumped back from the curb. Some even shouted and cursed at him.

There was a certain point, a moment, that Todd knew he was going to die today. It was when the pickup truck heading south jerked to the right and missed his bumper by a considerable berth, but the Chrysler 300 going north cut into the on-coming traffic of the passing lane and missed his car by a smaller gap than Todd's bumper had the Honda's, just seconds earlier. With this, the odds were stacked up too high for it *not* to happen today, Todd was certain.

He made it through the intersection safely and without a single bump to his car, rolling on through the narrowed street, but he knew his incredible luck wasn't going to last much longer. As he drove on through the now one-lane street that was crowded with the fat concrete columns supporting the Metromover rail above him, he wondered if the train might derail and plummet to the ground to crush him–a masterstroke of grisly luck to top off this wonderful day full of bullet holes and car chases.

"Talk to me. How you doing, buddy?" Alex asked from another galaxy.

Todd almost laughed.

He looked back and saw the Lincoln was mimicking Todd's zigzagging moves through the intersection, but in a much more cautious manner, breaking hard and cutting around the stopped Chrysler that was congesting traffic. The big car jerked to a stop and missed another oncoming vehicle, which blared its horn. The Lincoln was relentless, still playing catch-up but more importantly, confirming they were actually after him if they were just as aggressive in their pursuit as Todd was in his getaway.

"I'm good, but this guy is following my every move, dude. He is after me."

"Don't worry, it's almost over."

Todd blinked.

He didn't know what Alex meant by that, but he went along with it anyway, knowing he didn't have a choice. During their old friendly email exchanges, Alex had come off as a generally likable, easygoing guy. But the voice over the phone was like that of a commander and a leader, someone playing things out as he is seeing them. Like a chess master, perhaps, or a composer.

"Okay," Alex said. "Now you're going to hit a stop sign coming up; it's a one way T-junction. It's Biscayne North. I need you to make a wide turn left and get on Biscayne without stopping."

"What's going to happen?" Todd asked. The phone was becoming slippery and slimy in his clammy hand.

"It's going to be over, that's what."

Another look back in the mirror revealed the Lincoln gaining speed down the tight corridor of the street.

"Keep going, Todd," Alex encouraged.

Ahead, the street was empty save for a few meandering pedestrians, most with their heads down looking at their phones. Alex's stop sign—a bright lollipop against the sun—seemed to scream for Todd to stop.

Behind him, the Lincoln followed. With one final quick glance back before he blew past the stop sign, squealing tires and pulling left, Todd wondered if he was pressing his luck with another intersection and if this was where his time would finally catch up to him.

Todd braced himself for a deadly impact of some kind as he barreled through the wide intersection and turned left onto Biscayne, doing roughly forty mph past the stop sign, tires squealing. But when he looked down the street to his right, hair swirling and sweat running down his brow, he found the street was strangely vacant. Vacant except for the extra-large, two-ton Ford moving truck that was careening down the wide, clean street at a law-breaking speed…but at a safe distance from Todd.

Then—in that short moment—Todd thought he spotted an older, wrinkled face through the shining windshield, behind the wheel of that accelerating moving truck.

As Todd rounded Biscayne Boulevard north with plenty

of space between them, the two-ton Ford seemed to ignore the oncoming black Lincoln racing past the stop sign.

His pursuer's tires squealed in the same echoing banshee cry as Todd's big car when he ignored the stop sign. The Lincoln's engine roared. But the moving truck roared louder. In fact, the two vehicles sped through the crossing streets at the exact same moment, almost as if it they were aiming for each other.

The crash was magnificent and morbidly beautiful. The side panel of the Lincoln was crushed inward against the massive, unrelenting grill of the moving truck and was almost brought underneath of its hungry front end. Glass blew across the streets in every direction, like a cloudburst of fairy dust. The driver of the moving truck applied the brakes only a few feet from one of the columns elevating the Metromover train system. This created another echoing howl of rubber locking against pavement that squealed beneath the city structures like a sea monster just awoken from the abyss, only to be cut off when the truck sandwiched the car into the concrete column in another earth-shattering crunch of metal on metal.

It was about that time that Todd looked back to see the final seconds of the near-missed disaster. He laid on the brakes and pulled over in front of a tall, bureaucratic-looking building before looking back over his shoulder and out the window. The Lincoln's bent, shattered hood popped open as steam hissed from the front of the moving truck. Already, a dark liquid—Todd thought it might be transmission fluid—pooled outward from the wreckage on the hot pavement. Far off he heard a voice and realized it was Alex calling for him from his phone.

His breath was caught in his throat and he had to remind himself to start breathing again.

"Todd?"

"Ye...Yeah?"

"You all right?"

"Dude. Wha- What happened?"

"I took care of it."

Todd had now turned his whole body so he could peek out his driver-side window to see the results of the crash. The Lincoln was only a fragment of the car it once was. Surely, the driver was massively injured or, more than likely, crushed to death.

The passenger side door of the huge moving truck suddenly burst open. Slow at first but gaining speed, a white-haired elderly man spilled from the cab, landing on the pavement on his hands and knees and crouching like a beast. There was a gash at his temple and a dribble of blood ran down his face, but otherwise he appeared in fine condition…given the circumstances.

The old man shook off the daze and wiped away the blood from his face. Once he seemed to regain his composure, he scanned the streets before stealing a quick look at Todd. Todd knew he was looking directly at him; he could feel his piercing eyes. The elderly man nodded to him in a simple friendly recognition—then he did an incredible thing. For Todd, it was jolting.

He took off running.

But this wasn't "old-man running", that dawdling, clumsy trot. This was *running* running that defied logic and reason for someone in their late seventies. This was a sprint, a precise kind of Olympic dash. This was Usain Bolt running. This was Michael Johnson running. But with turbo boosters in their shoes. The few people on the street who had witnessed the crash and had their phones out issued audible gasps at the sight, as he took off back down Biscayne in a lightning sprint, before darting behind a building and disappearing. With their reaction, Todd felt a bit less lonely in the weirdness of his morning.

"Todd? Todd? You still there, buddy?" The phone seemed to be calling him from another world.

He didn't respond right away. He couldn't. But when he looked at the phone, he realized his hand was raised out the window.

Apparently, he had not only nodded to the old man, but he had waved back to him, too. Todd didn't even remember bringing his hand up, but he figured the southern hospitality he had adopted since living in the Keys had come out of him automatically.

Only, then it clicked. The old man hadn't looked directly at him and nodded for nothing—he had wanted to make sure Todd was looking at him when he took off running at his uncanny speed, making him aware that the Watchers still had his back.

He glanced again at the now-messy street corner with nary another car in sight coming from 3rd Street. Biscayne Boulevard had a solid flow of traffic heading his way from the south end of the street, unaware of the post-collision wreck they were about to see. He knew he should have taken off when he had the chance, but it wasn't until he saw those other cars coming that he got his ass moving again.

Todd pressed on the gas and rolled out of there.

To Alex, he said, "Yeah, man, I'm here."

"Look, I know you're shaken," Alex said in a much calmer voice than he'd used that day, "but you did great. Come to my place. I've got some rum in the blender, if you'd like. You probably need it."

"Yeah...I think I do," Todd admitted with a half sigh, half chuckle.

"Just remember what Plato said, my friend: 'the beginning is the most important part of the work'. And this is a beginning. Try to imagine how you will feel at the end."

With that mystical sendoff, he hung up.

*

Todd Freeman, Local Artist and Selfless Scavenger of Key West, Florida, slipped the phone into the cup holder of the console next to him. Distantly, around one of the towering buildings of downtown Miami, he heard wailing sirens, tipped off to the accident (already the third time he had heard and escaped those banshees today). This only fueled his desire to get to Alex and the Five and Dime. He thought he knew how to get there from his current place in the heart of the city, but he wanted to check the map anyway.

Though, as he reached for the printout in the passenger seat, he suddenly felt a faint warmth on his chest that began burning to a point of annoyance and confusion, to one of pain—searing pain—*very* quickly.

Out loud and to no one, he said, "What, am I having a heart attack now, too?" Thinking quick, he saw an open spot on the street and pulled over.

It was the coin in his pocket. The damned funny penny.

He pulled it out, the feel of it against his palm nowhere near as painful as his chest, even through his shirt. Yet, it was hot enough that his human reactionary side wanted to drop it, knowing it was hot, naturally reacting to the searing heat.

Except…he didn't.

He didn't drop it. Instead, he clutched it.

He let the coin's heat throb in his hand, almost in synch with his own heartbeat. And then…after just a few seconds…it *was* in synch.

Perfectly.

And for the shortest of moments, while the coin and his heartbeat fell into their joined rhythm, Todd felt really, *really* good. The fear not only melted away but seemed to evaporate in a cooling, internal wash that strongly reminded him of the Ecstasy he and Emma had taken in college over two decades ago, when they were dating and falling in love with each other for the first time. Or the sensation he felt all those years ago, driving through the majesty of the Keys for the first time, a new life and the bravery and the sincerity to accept the past awaiting him. It was only seconds long, but the moment was the overwhelming joy he'd felt when seeing Kyle just after his birth, eyes closed and crying. It was seeing the open and leaking eyes of the people he had helped who came into his studio as they wept, overwhelmed at the unexpected return of their lost treasure by such a big-hearted person.

But just as quickly as the powerful emotional surge had intensified, it began to subside. Tears had pooled in Todd's eyes, blurring his vision, forcing a quivering gasp as he tried not to break down at the intense beauty and love of those short seconds.

"What the fuck was that?" he gasped to no one.

Wiping the tears away and catching his breath, he slipped the now-cooling coin back into his shirt pocket and checked the side mirror. A small Toyota was about to cruise past him. After it did, he pulled back into the lane and continued on to Alex's shop buried somewhere in the city.

Todd didn't think he was losing his grip on sanity because of this. Yes, he'd had an incredibly traumatic, earth-shattering, sea change of a day, and he thought he was getting by pretty goddamned well after everything he had been through, but the fact that the coin was now, somehow, generating its own energy or emotional conduit into him was something for which he had very little bandwidth.

All he wanted was to meet with Alex, hand the coin over, and get it *the hell* out of his life. After that, it would be back to his painting life in Key West and searching the sands, but perhaps with a little more caution exercised for his stranger finds. Discovering crowbars used for murder is one thing, but this?

What *is* this?

He pulled the coin back out of his shirt pocket and glanced at it again, thinking how much *everything* had changed in the last six hours.

God, his studio! Who knew how much work he'd lost, or how much time he was going to lose in recovery and clean up, but the sooner he got on it, the quicker it would be finished.

Todd sighed, hard, and gazed east out his window and over

shimmering Biscayne Bay to Miami Beach and the ocean, to that far distant horizon where anything was possible, where massive clouds loomed on the cerulean blue sky like giant, fluffy mountains. An enormous super yacht cruised through the sparkling bay. A seagull squealed above him, cutting between the skyscrapers and high-rises.

Todd knew the truth. He knew as he clutched that damned penny and watched a pod of steel-colored pelicans cut the sky along the beach. He knew this wasn't going to stop at Alex's shop. He'd even said so himself—*this is a beginning.*

Who knew? Maybe that was a good thing. It had been before. Why couldn't it be this time?

One man's trash is another man's treasure?

Todd thought: *A funny penny saved is a funny penny earned.*

And what, exactly, was he earning?

A voice answered: *Magic.*

But he dismissed that. Not for disbelief, but for lack of endurance, tenacity, or nerve. For lack of any focus, ability or willingness to imagine what that entailed.

For now.

But maybe that one, *a funny penny earned*, was more fitting.

More fitting for the here and now. The Current.

And maybe, just maybe, he could find the magic in that penny too.

To Be Continued…

April 2008 - August 2020

AFTERWORD

Thank you for reading my novel, *Something Found: A Coin*. This is the first book in the planned Something Found Trilogy and I so hope you'll stick around for more. Todd's odyssey is just getting started and it's going to be wild. Like nothing I've ever done before.

This was a story idea (originally planned as one enormous 1100+ page tome of a book instead of a trilogy) that came to me fast and from extremely sad, but eventually uplifting, circumstances that unfolded in my life. In January 2008, the story of Todd, his artistry, his Floridian adventure, and everything to follow wasn't even on my horizons. Tragically, that was the month my brother died of an enlarged heart. Me being in California and strapped for cash, I couldn't make the funeral in Ohio on such quick, unexpected notice. 'Tis the life of a creative, and the sacrifices you make.

As a way to reconnect with family during the troubled time and reassure them I was in good health myself, I visited Florida with my wife. While there, we planned on taking a side trip to Miami and the Keys, two destinations that I had never been able to visit, not only on the multitude of Florida vacations my family and I took while growing up, but also in the two years I lived in Florida. Ridiculous, I know.

The car ride down was one of the highlights of the whole side trip and my first impressions of the Keys and Key West mirrored those of Todd's: this magical little island where artistic creativity flourished and was lauded. I hope I was able to capture the heart of the Keys and South Florida within these pages. And I hope the people of Key West and throughout the Florida Keys, and Miami, know how much of a positive impression you made on me. I wanted to paint your city in the same dreamy world that I cherished so in my short time I was there. Much love to the people of the Keys and South Florida. I hope I made you proud.

With this publication, I'm hoping to reinvigorate my readers and my own writing, to guide me back to continue down the path I originally started back in 2008 with Todd. I mean, he is named after my brother, after all. I should be able to finish it. It's like hanging out with him in some other world. I hope you liked hanging out with him, too.

There is a lot of work that goes into making a book, but even more so as an Indie Writer. I couldn't have made this happen without the following people: I want to thank my patient editor, Mike Robinson—the Mr. Utley to my Jimmy Buffett—for his guidance and ruthless cuts to my more droning lines of prose (*stubbump*). I want to also thank Bryan Miller for his proofread and for sharpening this sword to make it the best it can be. The team at Damonza.com has been nothing but a godsend for my covers and formatting, and I owe them a huge debt of gratitude. Thank you all so, so much. And a big thank you to all my beta readers as well. Thank you for reading!

And, of course, I have to give a special shoutout to all of my patrons on Patreon who've cheered me on and supported me over the years. They were also directly responsible for the making of this book through their financial backing. Thank you so much to Christina, Heather P., Stephanie, Tanya, Bethani, Jack and Janet, John, Angie, Brice, Liz, Heather M., and of course, Antionette. I couldn't have done this without you.

And as always, thank *you* so much for reading.

This book is fictional and the views expressed here are my own. Any and all errors in the text are mine as well.

August 11, 2020
Mission Viejo, California

Now that you have finished this book, could you please leave a review? Reviews help readers discover new books and new authors, while greatly increasing an author's chances of getting discovered, too. I hope you found this book to be a delight enough to return the favor for one. For authors, finding a new book review is as thrilling as finding a coin on a beach.

Connect:

Amazon.com/author/TroyAaronRatliff
Patreon.com/troyaaronratliff
Facebook: Troy Aaron Ratliff
Goodreads: Troy Aaron Ratliff
Instagram: @Trizzlepuffs
Twitter: @TARatliff

ABOUT THE AUTHOR

Troy Aaron Ratliff was born and raised in Hamilton, Ohio and has been autodidactic in various forms of writing, art, photography, music, quantum mechanics, and voice impersonations his entire life. When he's not writing, drawing, singing, or building his next beast, you can generally find him protecting the galaxy along side the forces of good, thwarting the diabolical plans of The Lizard People living in LA's sewers, indulging in high-intensity goat yoga, creating hypnotic soul-shifting art, dining with African bushmen, or trekking through the Amazon, but usually, he's flying over traffic deep within the bowels of Southern California on his winged fire-breathing rhinoceros.

Something Found: A Coin is his second novel.